THE KIDNEY SCAM

TRUE STORY OF BUSTING INDIA'S BIGGEST HUMAN ORGAN TRAFFICKING SCAM

KIRAN NIRVAN

An imprint of
Srishti Publishers & Distributors

Srishti Publishers & Distributors
A unit of AJR Publishing LLP
212A, Peacock Lane
Shahpur Jat, New Delhi – 110 049

editorial@srishtipublishers.com

First published by Bold,
an imprint of Srishti Publishers & Distributors in 2023

10 9 8 7 6 5 4 3 2 1

This is a work of non-fiction, based on the author's thorough research. Some events have been fictionalised for dramatic effect. While due care has been taken to verify all information at press time, any inadvertent miss brought to notice shall be updated in the subsequent editions.

Printed and bound in India

To everyone who's fighting against social evils.

And to the honest and hardworking medical workforce of our nation, striving day and night to save lives.

Acknowledgements

Among the many stories that we often come across, the story of the Kidney Scam was something that made us realize just how lucky and privileged we are to be able to sit on our desks and tables and write, while there is a faction of people out there, ready to sell even their vital organs just to make ends meet. And what is even more disturbing is the fact that there are people ready to prey on such underprivileged. But it is not why we chose to write the book. Showing how low we humans can stoop for greed and build a multi-million rupees organ trafficking scam is not the aim of this book.

Our focus is to show that despite this greed and a chunk of people trying to exploit, there will always be men and women who are ready to go through any extremes to restore our faith in humanity.

The Kidney Scam is the story of such selfless and daring people – nothing more, nothing less.

At the outset, we would like to extend our gratitude to Advocate Sarabjit Singh, whose help was pivotal for us in understanding the actual events of the scam and come up with a dramatised story and its characters inspired from reality.

We also thank Suhail Mathur of The Book Bakers Literary Agency for encouraging us to write in genres other than Military History. A special thanks to Mr Rajesh Rajput and

Mr Karan B Oberoi, two visionary men who strongly believe that this story deserves to be on screen and have been guiding us in that direction ever since they went through the story. Hopefully, this too shall fructify very soon.

We extend a heartfelt thanks to Arup Bose of Srishti Publishers who believed in this book, and our editor, Stuti Gupta, who gave this book a form that is worthy of being read.

Lastly, we can never thank our families and friends enough for their relentless support and comfort they provide us, so that we can enjoy doing what we do best – storytelling.

Kirandeep Singh
Nirvan Singh

Chapter 1

March, 2000. Amritsar.

A quick glance at the grim, starved faces of his wife Meeto and two children – five-year-old Rabi and six-year-old Sunny – left him worried once again. Hardial heaved a deep sigh as he pulled his cycle-rickshaw out. His small rented one-room house was just another such household in the crowded locality of *sabzi mandi* in the old city of Amritsar. He took out a small piece of cloth from under the seat of the rickshaw and started brushing off dust from his only source of income.

Starting as early as seven in the morning, Hardial visited all prominent tourist places in Amritsar in search of passengers. He had been pulling rickshaw for a living for the last ten years. His daily average earning hardly totalled to one hundred and fifty rupees, even when he toiled for more than twelve hours a day. People preferred auto-rickshaws now; they were cheaper and much faster.

'There is hardly anything left in the kitchen.' Meeto broke this grim news to Hardial while handing him a steel glass full of tea, which was more water and little milk, 'I'll have to manage with leftovers for today.'

'I will see what I can bring today,' Hardial replied, avoiding looking into Meeto's miserable eyes. The emptiness of her pierced ears – which once sported gold earrings, the ones Hardial had to sell to buy his own rickshaw – had begun to haunt him. It had been more than a year since Hardial had promised he would get Meeto's earrings back. The inability to fulfil his pledge made Hardial curse his stars. God knew he loved Meeto, and wished to give her all happiness in life. But despite all his efforts, he was helpless.

'The landlord came by when you were taking a bath. He says we must pay our outstanding rent within three days,' Meeto informed as Hardial sipped his tea in silence.

When she got no reply, she asked concerned, 'Why don't you let me find work?'

'I don't want to see you cleaning floors and utensils in households,' Hardial retorted. 'It's not why I had married you. I will manage.'

Placing the empty glass on the bricked floor of his small verandah, Hardial started cleaning the spokes of the front wheel of his rickshaw. Those were the only things shining in his life at that time. Meeto went inside to cook breakfast.

'You have magic in your hands,' Hardial commented as he ate, trying to lighten the atmosphere. 'These paranthas make me forget even my mother's cooking.'

'But you still love her more,' Meeto commented playfully while flipping a chapati on the griddle.

'I do, but I love you the most when you cook for me,' Hardial chuckled and leaned towards Meeto. 'You rule my heart, my dear wife.'

'Go away, you liar!' Meeto pushed Hardial and continued to roll out chapattis, but not before she tucked in the visible torn part of the cloth of her husband's turban, hiding the tear under other folds of the fabric.

Hardial took the tiffin and after giving a kiss to each of his sleeping children, he cycled towards the city. He usually got his passengers near Sangam Theatre, Bus Stand and 'Suraj Chanda Taara'[1]. As luck would have it, that day Hardial stumbled upon a man who had just got down from a bus coming from Ludhiana and wanted to go to Ranjit Avenue. Riding to the colony which was almost ten kilometres away from the bus stand would fetch Hardial a minimum of forty rupees. Well aware that all passengers bargain, he asked for fifty rupees. As he had thought, the passenger finally settled for forty. It took Hardial more than thirty minutes of constant paddling to reach the destination at Ranjit Avenue.

When Hardial turned his rickshaw back towards the city, a faint noise caught his attention. Like a cellphone ringing close by. On careful inspection, Hardial saw a big black device stuck in the crack at the edge of his rickshaw's seat. He fished it out only to see a dazzling, brand new Motorola handset. It was a newly-launched expensive product. A number of thoughts crossed Hardial's mind, but an honest believer in the Guru's teachings, he decided to give it back to the owner.

He drove back to Ranjit Avenue and handed over the device to the passenger. He offered Hardial money for his honesty, but Hardial simply folded his hands and drove away. Despite all the problems at home, Hardial chose to live with dignity.

Despite the good start to the day, Hardial's total earning couldn't surpass two hundred rupees. But at least he now

---

1 *Name of a single complex having three theatres*

had some money to buy grocery. The landlord's approaching deadline was an overwhelming worry at the back of his mind.

This entailed that he had to work harder the next day.

Hardial managed to earn three hundred rupees the next day, but it was only one-fourth of the outstanding rent of three months. He knew that his landlord would not extend the term of his accommodation without the entire amount this time. With no visible solution in sight, he decided to leave everything to fate.

On the third and final day of the landlord's ultimatum, Hardial had managed to earn two hundred rupees till afternoon. At around two, a starved and tensed Hardial pulled over his rickshaw at his friend Nathu's tea stall outside Chitra cinema, his usual spot for lunch.

'Make a strong one for me,' said Hardial as he took out chapattis wrapped in a piece of cloth with mango pickle. He began to eat hurriedly, without exchanging another word with Nathu.

'Is everything alright?' Nathu enquired.

When there was no reply from Hardial, Nathu put aside his saucepan and walked towards him. 'I asked you something, Hardial,' Nathu said while nudging him. 'Why aren't you answering?'

Hardial broke into tears at Nathu's questioning and told him everything.

'It is okay. You can shift to my place for now. We will find a solution later,' Nathu consoled Hardial. Nathu's supporting words and a pat on the back gave Hardial some relief.

Sitting on a bench in one corner of the tea stall, Chandu heard their conversation carefully. A medium built, mid-aged

Chandu was a commissioning agent at a local blood bank that sold blood to patients in need. A typical businessman who always looked for profit, it was his job to lure poor persons in need of money to sell blood. He didn't want to let this opportunity go away, so he quickly approached Hardial as Nathu got busy with his work.

'How much for dropping me at Sultanwind road, Sardaarji?' Chandu, a Bihari by birth, asked in a poor Punjabi dialect while setting his thick, oiled hair behind his ears with one hand.

'Fifteen rupees,' Hardial replied as he wiped his face with a small cloth wrapped around his neck.

Chandu hopped on to the seat without bargaining and Hardial drove his rickshaw towards Sultanwind Gate.

'How much do you earn in a day, Sardaarji?' Chandu asked.

An already frustrated Hardial didn't reply at first, but when asked again, he said, 'Not much. Around one hundred and fifty rupees.'

'That's too less,' Chandu replied, trying to sympathize with Hardial.

Chandu continued to enquire about Hardial and his family as he saw a potential donor in front of him. Poor and innocent Hardial kept telling him everything. When Chandu had made Hardial comfortable in the conversation, he offered him to sell his blood. He knew that Hardial was in dire need of money and he would not refuse.

'How can one *sell* blood? Shouldn't it be *donated*?' Hardial questioned.

'O Sardaarji! It is also a sort of donation. The only difference is that they provide you money for your well-being. For a normal blood group, a person gets two hundred rupees per bottle and for a rare blood group, it is double!' Chandu replied. Then he started teaching Hardial about different blood groups. Hardial was aware about his blood group, thanks to the treatment of an ailment in the past.

'You're a B-Negative, Sardaarji! You can get really good money,' Chandu shouted in excitement. Hardial, still reluctant to *sell* blood, didn't show any signs of pleasure.

'What happened, Sardaarji? Don't worry, I also donate blood regularly. It doesn't take a toll on our bodies. You'll be fine,' Chandu said, showing Hardial needle marks on both his arms.

Hardial continued sitting on his rickshaw, lost in a sea of thoughts. All his poverty flashed in front of his eyes in the next few minutes. He put a hand inside his pocket and took out all the money he had earned in the last two days. It was only six hundred rupees. He looked towards the sun with a deep grimace. It had already started its journey towards the horizon. The thought that he won't be able to pay the rent by evening got into his head. Marred by circumstances and with no other visible solution, Hardial succumbed and headed straight towards the blood bank at Sultanwind road with Chandu. Within no time, Hardial was asked to lie on a bed and his arm was strapped. The nurse gave him a soft ball to hold and press to regulate blood flow, as she prepared a needle. It wasn't difficult for the nurse to locate his vein on the skinny arm.

After one bottle had been taken out, Hardial insisted that he could give more. Chandu convinced the nurse, and finally, two bottles of blood were taken out of Hardial's body.

To Hardial's surprise and amazement, he was given eight hundred rupees, four boiled eggs and a bunch of bananas in return. He ate the eggs and kept the bunch of bananas in a polybag for his children and Meeto. Chandu received his commission too, which Hardial remained unaware of.

After mustering some strength, he headed towards his rickshaw. With more than required money in his pocket for paying off outstanding rent, Hardial paddled away. He stopped outside the landlord's house and paid off his rent.

On his way home, he bought grocery from the remaining money and treats for his children after a long time. He kept the blood donation incidence from Meeto. To him, a good night's sleep was all that mattered that day.

Before leaving the blood bank, Chandu had thrown Hardial an option to donate blood every month and the benefits of making easy money through simple donation had already taken the best of Hardial.

A month passed and Hardial found himself outside the blood bank yet again. He wasn't earning any better from his rickshaw pulling job anyway.

'Ah! There you are, my friend Sardaarji!' Chandu exclaimed with fake happiness on seeing Hardial. 'Ready to donate blood again?'

Hardial simply nodded and ended up donating one bottle.

It was when he was feasting on the boiled eggs when Chandu came and sat beside him.

'Let's get some tea from Nathu?' Chandu offered, clearly trying to start a conversation.

'Some other day, Bhai. I am already full. Thank you!' Hardial replied, looking in a hurry to get back to his job. But when an adamant Chandu insisted, Hardial agreed. It had taken only two visits for Chandu to befriend Hardial and when he thought that Hardial trusted him, a shrewd Chandu threw bait again.

'Now it is time to earn more, Sardaarji. For how long will you keep pleasing yourself with a few hundred rupees?' said Chandu as they sipped tea at Nathu's tea stall.

'How?' Hardial asked, knowing well that Chandu was clever to offer choices that fetched money.

'Come with me, I'll take you to Raju. Only he can tell how. But rest assured, it's much more money than what you get from donating blood.' Chandu's eyes shone as he spoke.

Hardial agreed in his innocence and Chandu took him to Jhakhar Hospital, one of the well-known multi-speciality hospitals in Amritsar.

Hardial had never been to such a big hospital before – never had the cause, or the money. The view of the towering main building of the multi-storeyed hospital against a pale blue sky left Hardial mesmerized. Even though he had always been scared of hospitals and clinics, he trailed behind Chandu nonchalantly as they went inside. Chandu asked Hardial to wait at the reception and went inside to look for Raju. He came back with a fair, medium-built man with thick spectacles.

Sitting in the canteen area, Chandu, Hardial and Raju talked in detail about something that Raju thought could help Hardial in earning money. Little did Hardial know that it was all but a part of a plan, a trap being set up by Chandu and Raju.

'What I'm going to tell you might sound confusing and scary, but it isn't what it looks like. The truth is that many people have benefitted from it,' Raju said.

'Tell me and I'll do it. Any job is suitable for me if it pays more than I currently earn,' Hardial said.

'No no, it's not a job offer!' Raju pretended to laugh and continued, 'It's a one-time thing and you'll earn enough.' A confused Hardial exchanged looks with Chandu, who told him to listen further.

'There are many organs in our body which are extra. There is no need for them. A person can live a healthy life even after removal of these extra organs, while that extra organ can be donated to someone else,' Raju explained. 'Kidneys, for example, are one of them. There are two in our bodies, while a person can live normally with one also.'

Hardial looked confused.

'Let's cut to the chase,' an impatient Chandu barged in. 'If you sell one of your kidneys, you will get five lakh rupees in return.'

'That's huge!' Hardial exclaimed.

'Yes, it is,' Chandu said. He leaned towards Hardial and whispered, 'Even the monthly interest of this amount will be more than what you are earning right now.'

Hardial, who was still in disbelief, was at a loss for words. This was too much money for him. He was perplexed on discovering this information. On one side was an offer of a lifetime which could end his miserable life, and on the other side was the risk to his health. He wanted to choose the first option, but was also worried. What if the operation didn't go well? He won't even be able to pull his rickshaw to make ends meet.

'I know what you're thinking. Let me end that worry of yours too,' Raju said as he stood up and tucked out his shirt from one side to show Hardial an old, healed incision mark on his abdomen. 'I have also donated one. Do I look unhealthy to you?'

Hardial was surprised, and a little more convinced on seeing this. Even then, Hardial wished to learn more about the process. Chandu and Raju took Hardial to the office of the doctor who performed surgeries for kidney removal. An assurance from the doctor convinced Hardial a little more.

'There is nothing to worry. Good luck,' said the doctor as they walked out of his room.

'I will think about it,' Hardial ensured Chandu.

Chandu and Raju grinned as Hardial left the hospital premises.

Hardial called it a day and went home. He ran his gaze through his house, carefully examining everything. It was only natural for him to think how unlucky he was, as he couldn't even provide his family with the very basic needs. Meeto sensed that something was disturbing Hardial and tried to calm him. But despite the turmoil in his mind and heart, Hardial didn't tell her anything. It was hard for him to find sleep that night. He kept on calculating what all he could buy with five lakh rupees and finally narrowed down to an auto-rickshaw. He thought his dreams could come true. Keeping in mind a better future for his family, he finally decided to donate his kidney in return for the offered money. Somewhere in the middle of the night, Hardial fell asleep.

***

'You will have to stay at the hospital for an entire month until you fully recover. The hospital will take care of your treatment and expenses incurred on the same,' Raju explained to Hardial the next morning at Jhakhar Hospital.

'What about the money?' Hardial asked.

Raju's hand reached for his pocket and he took out an envelope containing five thousand rupees.

'Here's your advance! The rest of the money will be paid immediately after the operation,' Chandu said as Raju gave the envelope to Hardial.

'But there is one problem, Chandu. I cannot tell the truth to my wife, otherwise she will not let me donate my kidney,' Hardial said.

'We will take care of that. Chandu will visit your home tomorrow and hand over these five thousand rupees to her. He will cook up a story that you have been appointed as a labourer in a construction company in Chandigarh for one month,' Raju said.

Hardial nodded in agreement.

All went as planned and Chandu visited Hardial's house to tell Meeto the false story. She fell for it.

Hardial was admitted in the OPD the very next day. In the afternoon, Hardial was given some paperwork as formalities, which he signed without reading. The Authorisation Committee approved the donation immediately. A surgery was scheduled the same evening. A group of surgeons successfully removed his kidney, which was transplanted into the recipient on 10 May 2000.

When Hardial woke up the next day, he felt a stinging pain in his abdomen. But good post-operative care rendered him satisfied.

Chandu often came to visit him in the course of the next few days and gave him another forty-five thousand rupees in instalments. Everything went as had been mentioned to Hardial till the next two weeks. But things worsened thereafter.

By now partially recovered, Hardial was shifted to a private villa at White Avenue in the middle of the night, citing administrative issues at the hospital. It was only the next morning, when Hardial saw four other patients there who had sold their kidney just like Hardial, that he came to develop a suspicion that he had been played. All others present there shared the same fate. It was from these other patients that he came to know that Chandu and Raju were middlemen of a kidney trade. It was their job to lure poor people like Hardial and others and sell their kidney to the rich to earn money from commissions.

Sensing that his future and his dreams were in jeopardy, Hardial asked the attendants there for a phone call or a meeting with Chandu and Raju. But his incessant requests reaped no results. He then demanded his remaining money, but again, his requests fell on deaf ears. Circumstances seemed to solidify Hardial's fear every day that he might have fallen for a fraud. He wanted to escape from the villa, but he was forcefully stopped at the gate. A furious Hardial gathered some strength and vandalised some medical equipment in rage. This act led the attendants to throw him out of the villa in a partially-recovered state immediately, with threats that if he demanded anything, he and his family would face dire consequences.

A dejected Hardial managed to reach home, where Meeto panicked on seeing him unwell. She assisted him to get inside and put him into bed. Hardial disclosed everything to Meeto, handing her the forty-five thousand rupees. Tears filled the poor couple's eyes. Dreams went back to remain just dreams once again. Sleepless nights followed as the family inched towards a miserable future.

Meeto took good care of Hardial for the next few weeks and the money soon exhausted in his medication. Circumstances forced Hardial to fall back to his job of pulling a rickshaw, but he was physically too weak to do so. Inability to work filled Hardial with rage and he decided to lodge a complaint at the local police station against Chandu, Raju and Jhakhar Hospital, unaware that he was going to set one of the country's biggest investigations in motion.

Chapter 2

'Oh no! Not again!' Kirti cupped her forehead when Dr Baljit Verma – the professor of anatomy at Medical College, Amritsar – entered the class for another lecture on behalf of his colleague, who was on leave that day. Both Rahul and Gurkirat chuckled at an exhausted Kirti's displeasure as the students stood up to greet the teacher. Kirti batted her eyes at them in return. All students of MBBS third year, they comprised one of the most-famed trio in the entire college, since the very start of the course.

Kirti sported a perfect bob cut, and was known amongst peers for being a little outspoken. A local resident of Amritsar, she never could get along well with other girls in college. Rahul, who had liked her from the very first day of their course, used this opportunity to befriend her. She too liked his company, because he would never complain about her blunt and forthright behaviour and stood beside her in every situation.

Rahul had come all the way from Bihar to pursue his degree at Amritsar's famous Medical College. He lived in the hostel and shared his room with Gurkirat, an open bearded Sikh lad hailing from Jalandhar. Notwithstanding the ethnic differences, both had turned out to be best buddies.

'I am starving! And there's a whole lecture between me and my favourite food,' Kirti mumbled. Rahul let out a muffled laugh as she slyly opened her tiffin, only to see two small chapattis and a handful of scrambled eggs!

'Urgh,' she silently growled. 'How can mom do this to me and my appetite? How is this going to satisfy my hunger?'

She rolled a chapatti and hogged it in two bites, while giving the other one to Rahul. Gurkirat, a baptised Sikh, chose to focus on the lecture instead. The two extra hours of the same subject's lecture left everyone in class bored. Almost all the students were sleeping with open eyes. Nobody even cared to respond or ask questions. And when finally the bell rang, everyone scrambled out of the class in a horde. Hostellers made their way towards the mess and other students rushed towards the college canteen for lunch.

'I don't know why I'm so hungry today!' Kirti exclaimed as she slung her backpack on one of her shoulders. Its weight seemed to pull her skinny shoulder down.

'Extra lectures can really suck the energy out of you,' Gurkirat said.

'Guys, let's grab something special for lunch today,' Kirti said to the boys, who were about to walk towards the hostel's mess.

'And what's the special thing?' Rahul stopped and asked, delighted at the prospect of having lunch with Kirti.

'Popular Bakery!' she replied at once.

'As you wish!' said Rahul and started to walk towards the exit gate instead.

'Do you need an invitation?' both said in unison while looking back towards Gurkirat, who hadn't moved.

'Why the bakery?' Gurkirat, unhappy at the idea of eating at a bakery, rolled his eyes before giving up and joining the other two. A brawny, six feet towering Gurkirat could only be satiated with a proper lunch. Those bakery snacks hardly made a difference to him. But friends never abandon other friends and he knew it well.

The Medical College had two entry and exit points, one each in the front and rear. Where the main gate was at the front and was used as the primary entrance and exit, the smaller one at the rear of the college was used by the students to visit the in-campus hospital. There were a couple of shops at the opposite side of the road in front of the main gate, including a book shop, a tailor's shop, a dhaba and the famous Popular Bakery. It was always crowded with students as well as regular customers addicted to the freshly-baked crunchy cream rolls.

No sooner did the trio enter the bakery, elbowing their way through other customers, than Kirti joyfully started admiring the various snacks laid inside the glass counter. Before Gurkirat could give his say, Rahul went ahead and ordered whatever Kirti pointed at. When the delicacies arrived, both Kirti and Rahul filled their plates and started munching, without even realizing that there was someone else with them. Gurkirat scavenged whatever was left and started eating. Often just an invisible accomplice, Gurkirat would let Rahul and Kirti spend time. His only job was to rescue his best friend Rahul in case awkward situations showed up.

'I'm going to order more,' said Kirti.

'You've won a lottery or something?' Gurkirat commented and Kirti winked and gestured him to shift his gaze towards the cash counter where Ratan Lal, an administrative officer of the college, was paying for his order. Still unmarried and in his late forties, Ratan Lal always went weak in his knees in Kirti's presence, and she knew it well. Mischievous as she was, she went up to Ratan Lal at once.

'Good afternoon, sir!' Kirti said from behind his back.

'Kirti! Good... good afternoon,' Ratan Lal turned to her and answered, carefully brushing off thin strands of hair to one side of his almost bald head. A broad, ear-to-ear smile appeared on his round face. 'What brings you here?'

'It's my parents' anniversary today,' Kirti lied through her teeth and pointed towards Rahul and Gurkirat, who immediately looked away to avoid eye contact with Ratan Lal. Moreover, he would have seen them laughing.

'Congratulations then! It is a great day,' said the aged bachelor while moving one step closer towards Kirti. She took out some loose cash from the pocket of her jeans and pretended to look distressed while counting, prompting Ratan Lal to ask her if there was a problem.

'I think I dropped some money somewhere.' Kirti grimaced.

'It will be a disgrace if I tell this to my friends now. Guess I'll have to call it off.'

'Oh Kirti, why are you worrying about such a petty issue when I am here? This one is on me now,' Ratan Lal proudly said and paid on Kirti's behalf.

'I was hoping if someday we can grab a...' before Ratan Lal could play his card, Kirti thanked him and hurriedly walked back to her friends, leaving poor Ratan Lal wondering if he had been fooled once again.

'You are unbelievable!' Rahul told Kirti. 'How do you make him fall for this every single time?'

'Charm, my friend,' a proud Kirti replied with a joyful smile, leaving Rahul admiring her in silence for a moment. Gurkirat looked away towards the road and saw people gathering in a circle around something.

'I think someone has met with an accident,' Gurkirat said.

'Or it could be a street fight,' replied Rahul, while looking towards the crowd. 'Let's go!'

Gurkirat and Kirti continued eating, while Rahul immediately went out and walked towards the crowd curiously, still holding his half-finished cream roll. He elbowed his way through the crowd, only to see that a seemingly weak rickshaw puller lying unconscious in the middle of the road. Crimson-red patches below his chest spread outwards on his mud-stained shirt.

Rahul threw away the rest of his cream-roll, immediately pushed the onlookers away and checked his pulse. Upon realizing that the rickshaw puller was still alive, he shouted at people to call for his friends from the bakery. Gurkirat and Kirti came running to Rahul on hearing the cries.

From sprinkling water on the victim's face to all other first-aid measures, the trio tried them all, but the rickshaw puller remained unconscious and unresponsive. Assessing the gravity of the situation, without wasting any time, Gurkirat put his brawny built to use and carried the unconscious rickshaw puller to Medical College Hospital in his arms. The victim's body felt too light, as if there was no mass left inside of him. He was taken to the emergency ward and within no time, the medical treatment began.

'This man has recently donated his kidney,' Rahul said as they waited outside the emergency ward after senior doctors took charge of the patient. 'I saw his half-healed incision wound when I tried to examine the source of the crimson red patches on his shirt. I don't understand who discharged him without complete recovery and allowed him to do such a tedious job in such a condition.'

'That's really depressing!' Kirti exclaimed. 'Such negligence could cost him his life.'

'Let's ask him once he's up,' Gurkirat said.

A dedicated team of doctors and interns worked continuously for the next three hours to save the critical patient and finally succeeded in their efforts. The rickshaw puller finally regained consciousness. Rahul, Kirti and Gurkirat requested the doctors to let them meet him.

The rickshaw puller introduced himself as Hardial and thanked the trio for helping him. Rahul asked Hardial about his incision wound and found him beating around the bush, clearly dodging their questions regarding kidney donation. Hardial was reminded of the broker's threats and refused to admit anything. Hardial's behaviour raised suspicion in Gurkirat's mind. 'So, you're telling us this scar isn't from a kidney removal operation? Should we get it checked?'

'Let him rest, Gurkirat,' Rahul nudged Gurkirat and gestured everyone to move outside.

'You don't know Punjabis as well as I do,' Gurkirat said, not moving a bit. 'He's clearly lying. I just want to know why.'

Hardial finally succumbed to Gurkirat's stubbornness. Moreover, he knew that there was no point in lying as these medical students were smart enough to find out the truth anyway.

'You are the second person I am telling this, other than my wife. But please don't tell anyone else,' Hardial spoke painfully in a faint voice, struggling to fold his hands. Kirti and Rahul stepped closer to his bed as Hardial managed to put his ordeal into words. He laid bare all the happenings that had brought him where he was. Heartbroken and miserable, Hardial couldn't help stop his tears from rolling down his bony cheeks.

'You should have gone to the police!' Gurkirat retorted. It was one of those rear occasions when Gurkirat spoke more than Kirti and Rahul. He was clearly upset on hearing Hardial's story.

'I had lodged a police complaint, but nothing happened,' Hardial replied, while trying to sit and lean on a pillow. Kirti bent forward and gestured him to keep lying on the bed as he spoke. 'Who listens to us meagre beings anyway? Police often doesn't move until you grease their hands.'

There was nothing the three could say or do to console Hardial. Suggesting that he should rest for a while, the trio walked outside. Hardial thought it best to take a nap for a while. The three friends entered into a discussion on the matter that Hardial had just disclosed. They wondered how this could happen in the holy city of Amritsar. As medical students, they were well aware of the formalities and laws with regards to organ donation and they could only reach at one conclusion – something wrong was going on somewhere.

'I think we should talk to the college authorities regarding this,' Kirti suggested.

'We should,' Rahul seconded her suggestion.

'No,' Gurkirat said at once, confusing Kirti and Rahul. 'We cannot just walk up to anyone and discuss this. It could possibly be illegal organ trade, and honestly, people involved in this must have their roots everywhere. Besides, if no action has been initiated by the police yet, I believe it's because they have been ordered not to.'

'Why are you so suspicious of everything?' Rahul commented.

'Because I apply my mind, dumbass!' Gurkirat retorted and then turned towards Kirti and continued, 'Who will you inform anyway? The Principal? FYI, he heads the authorisation committee which approves organ transplant cases. If an organ transplant had taken place in Jhakhar hospital, who do you think would have approved it?'

'So, you're saying Principal sir is involved?' Rahul said.

'No, I'm not saying this!' Gurkirat was slightly annoyed at Rahul's inability to understand the situation. He said a little loudly, 'All I'm saying is, I sense something bigger. If this man has been fooled, it requires breach at multiple levels! Since the process of organ transplant is full of complicated steps, legal formalities, etc., it could be possible that even the authorisation committee has been fooled. And do you think the Principal would not try to hide this failure?'

'Principal sir is a nice man. He will listen, I'm sure,' Kirti was hopeful.

'It's too early to do anything,' Gurkirat suggested. 'This has legal implications. Besides, that man has received life threats. We cannot put his life at further risk. Don't act impulsively.'

'Gurkirat is right! We have to be very cautious,' said Kirti.

'At least she understands,' Gurkirat said, passing a look of disappointment towards Rahul.

'So, what should we do?' asked Rahul. 'We have to help this poor man.'

'Firstly, let's inform his wife about his condition,' Gurkirat said. 'Then maybe we can talk to some lawyer or activist, if they'd like to help Hardial.'

Gurkirat stayed back with Hardial as he slept, while Kirti and Rahul brought Meeto with them from Hardial's house. Meeto, a little shaken up in the beginning, thanked the students for their help and took her seat beside Hardial to watch over him. The students left, assuring Meeto that they would come back the next day. Sensing the terrible nature of this matter, these alarmed students started looking for options.

'Where to go first?' Gurkirat asked while they walked out of the campus.

'I think we should contact a lawyer first,' replied Kirti.

'Now? It's too late already. I have to head back home,' Kirti said, looking at her digital wrist watch.

'Even we have to work on Dr Verma's assignments,' Rahul said worriedly, almost reminding himself that he had not even started making one.

'Let's catch up tomorrow then,' Gurkirat suggested.

'Sure,' Kirti said while looking for an auto-rickshaw. Out of nowhere, she decided to stop a rickshaw-puller instead. 'Meanwhile, let me find out if my family knows any advocate who can help.'

'Sure. But no details, okay? We'll only tell enough to enable the advocate to guide us further. We cannot trust anyone,' warned Gurkirat as Kirti hopped on the rickshaw, reassuring them with a thumbs-up.

The next day, the trio decided to miss out on all classes, citing different reasons to their teachers. They went to the office of a lawyer, referred to Kirti by one of her cousins.

Upon meeting with the lawyer, Gurkirat carefully meted out details without disclosing any names and simply said that they had stumbled upon someone who had been a victim of organ fraud. The lawyer told them that solid proof would be required before anything could be concluded. Assuring the lawyer that they were gathering proofs and would come back soon with details, they left the office.

'He thought we were just fooling around,' a disheartened Rahul said. 'If we had told him the details, he would have thought we were genuine guys trying to do the right thing. And see, he simply showed us out.'

'When will you learn anything? Why can't you assess from simple details?' Gurkirat almost scolded Rahul. 'Remember, all paperwork for organ donations like affidavits and declarations are done by advocates. And in Hardial's case, either all the paperwork would be fake or not exist. If it's fake, only an advocate could have faked it.'

'Do you suspect your own family this way?' Rahul mumbled almost inaudibly and grinned.

'Gurkirat is right! We cannot trust anyone,' Kirti concluded and Rahul's smile vanished as he tried to look serious.

'Then why did we even come here?' Rahul questioned Kirti.

'To explore all possibilities,' replied Gurkirat.

'I have another option,' Kirti said as the trio walked on one side of the road, towards the college.

'There's this political leader whose party is currently in opposition. She can help,' Kirti said. 'She is a social activist as well.'

'You're very sharp,' Rahul commented.

'I read newspapers. Can you spell out one?' Kirti rudely got back at him. Gurkirat grinned at Rahul's failure to impress her with his usual stupid remarks. Rahul playfully hit him in the back.

Nirmala Devi had been a political leader for more than three decades now. She was known in the city for raising her voice on issues concerning human rights. With this as a backdrop, she never let go of any opportunity to attack the opposite party. There was hardly anyone from the opposition who didn't respect or like this white-haired, witty yet humble old lady. Kirti, Rahul and Gurkirat took their chance, and even when the possibility of her meeting with them was grim, they decided to go to her party's head office.

To their surprise and luck, she was present in the office and informed her PA to let the students meet her in the next fifteen minutes. The students waited and fifteen minutes stretched to two hours. Finally, they were allowed to go inside to meet Nirmala. Initially mesmerized by her presence and swooning over the fact that they were seeing Nirmala Devi in person, Gurkirat took the matter in his hands and narrated to her the story, minus the details – the way they had done in the lawyer's office.

'Seems to be a serious matter,' Nirmala Devi said. Everyone remained silent as she reached for her pen and wrote something on a piece paper on her desk.

'You need not go anywhere else now. I will take care of everything. I will raise this issue and put pressure on the government, until they catch the culprits,' Nirmala Devi said in a suave tone.

'Thank you, ma'am,' the students said in unison.

'You just go and bring the victim to me. We will plan and take him in front of the Chief Minister's office. We will protest. I will gather all my workers. If he will not listen, we will jam the roads,' she said.

Before Rahul or Kirti could say anything, Gurkirat barged in and assured Nirmala Devi that they would bring the victim and took her leave on his friends' behalf as well.

'What was that?' Kirti asked, baffled at Gurkirat's suddenness.

'I don't think she would be helpful in any way,' Gurkirat commented.

'Why? Now don't tell me you suspect her to be involved as well! You're just watching too much TV these days,' Rahul let out a nonsensical rant.

'She just promised us all that because she wants to garner political attention with such cases. Don't you see that will only improve her current position in the party?' Gurkirat said, while pointing his finger towards the gate of Nirmala's residence, where a convoy had just stopped. A cabinet minister stepped out of a white Tata Safari.

'A cabinet minister of the current government is here to meet her. If she has such reach in the ruling party, why would she suggest protesting in front of the CM's office? She is powerful enough to get this case solved in minutes, with or without meeting the victim,' Gurkirat shared his assessment in one go.

'How can you be so right?' Kirti commented while Rahul rolled his eyes in visible envy.

'Our Mr Analyst has negated all our options. I don't think we can find anyone now,' Rahul said, as they walked away from Nirmala Devi's head office premises.

'There is one person who I think can help us,' Gurkirat said after the trio had walked silently for a while. 'Manjit Singh. He is a distant relative of mine. He is an advocate and a social activist too. And above all, he lives in Amritsar,' Gurkirat told them.

'Why did you keep him a mystery till now?' questioned the other two at once.

'Because,' Gurkirat paused for a bit and continued, 'he's a bit odd. I don't even know if he will listen to us.'

'We can only find out once we meet him,' Kirti said.

A little push by the other two led Gurkirat to call his father from a PCO and ask him for Manjit Singh's address.

***

Colors of the evening sky began to spread. It was already late, but the frustration of all three of them led them to continue their efforts for a bit longer. Any ray of hope was welcome at that juncture. And besides, as medical students, they considered it their duty to help someone wronged by the very profession they were preparing themselves for. So, they decided to pay a visit to Manjit Singh and found themselves outside his house in the next half hour.

Rahul rang the doorbell and a short, turbaned man, sporting short boxed beard sprinkled with evenly distributed white hair opened the door. Lowering his spectacles, he looked at the trio with a questioning gaze. Gurkirat at once introduced himself and half-reluctantly, Manjit Singh allowed the three of them to enter.

'What makes you think I can help you?' A serious-looking Manjit asked in a monotonous, plain tone.

'I... I was told by Papaji that you do such kind of work,' Gurkirat managed to answer.

'Not anymore,' Manjit said bluntly as he walked up to open the door, gesturing the trio to leave.

'But chachaji, is there some problem?' Gurkirat asked.

'Yes,' an expressionless Manjit said, without looking at any of them. 'You're wasting my time and yours as well. You should go, study. Many wrong things keep happening to many people in this city. You can't stop all of it, can you?'

This came as a surprise for the students who had come to Manjit with so much hope. They looked towards each other, but didn't know what to say. Kirti and Rahul gestured Gurkirat to ask him once more. When Gurkirat tried to convince Manjit, he asked the three to leave. Disheartened and completely exhausted, Gurkirat and Rahul dropped Kirti at her home and went back to the hostel. The day's hard work had reaped no results, and they could not even meet Hardial. How would they face him, they thought.

None of the three could sleep that night. Failure had taken a toll on them.

Chapter 3

A goods carrier rammed into Manjit's car from the co-driver's side when he was crossing the intersection at around eleven in the night. The car toppled over several times, but Manjit sustained minor injuries. His wife was severely injured, though. He struggled to crawl out and pulled his wife out of the damaged car. He laid her bloodstained, unconscious body on the footpath and ran towards the road. The truck was still there with headlights on. The driver had long escaped. A panicked Manjit, whose turban had fallen on his shoulders from the impact, continuously waived to passersby, but none of them stopped. After about fifteen minutes, a car stopped and Manjit and his wife were taken to the hospital. A stretcher took his wife to the emergency ward as Manjit waited outside.

'I am sorry. We couldn't save her,' a doctor came out after half an hour and broke the news to Manjit. The words rang inside his ears for a while.

Manjit woke up in the middle of the night, breathing heavily, drenched in sweat. It was the same nightmare once again. He gulped an entire glass of water. The accident from five years ago still haunted him. An anonymous caller had told Manjit that the intent was only to teach him a lesson. His wife's death was collateral damage, but it had left Manjit shattered. Due to lack of evidence, the case was closed. A local mafia had destroyed him, only because he had helped a poor family get justice. It was a dirty world and those in power had corrupted those who were meant to exercise their power. A common man could only survive if he did not intervene with them. Therefore Manjit, in spite of being an advocate and a social activist, had given up. He had stopped carrying out social work or practicing law ever since this saddening episode.

Hardial's story had reminded Manjit about his own case, which was almost similar to it. It brought back the bitter memories, the reason why Manjit had denied his help. He had nothing to lose now, but his wife's death had rendered him weak. He could not sleep that night. He kept tossing and turning. He did not want to get involved in any such case anymore.

The next day, Hardial was discharged from the Medical College hospital. Rahul, Kirti and Gurkirat arranged for him to go back to his house. Over the previous few days, owing to Hardial's simplicity and honesty, the trio had connected with him on a personal level and assured every help to Meeto and Hardial till Hardial's complete recovery. Young, enthusiastic and taken aback by the revelation of such a scam, they decided to gather evidence on their own to support Hardial's case, hoping their honest deeds might get him justice.

A casual evening trip to Jhakhar hospital to find some leads reaped nothing beneficial. None of them could find access to authorization committee's office and their requests to pay a casual visit there fell on deaf ears. Convincing them could raise suspicion, they knew too well, so they dropped the idea. Finally, after taking the address from Hardial, the trio visited the safe house where he had been kept.

It was a huge independent villa with security guards manning the gate. Kirti straightaway walked up to the guards and stated a conversation. At first, the guards kept on talking, but when her questions became more direct in nature, they asked Kirti to go away. The students were done trying everything they could to gather information on the illegal organ trade, but hadn't found any solid proof.

Fed up of running aimlessly, they knew that the only person who could help them was Manjit and they had to get back to him. Incessant ringing of the doorbell woke Manjit Singh early in the morning. Still half asleep, when he opened the door, he was confused to see Kirti, Rahul, Gurkirat and Hardial with his wife and two little children. The students took the poor family to Manjit's house, hoping that their condition might melt Manjit. But the adamant lawyer was still in no mood to help them.

'I have already told you that I can't do anything,' Manjit said, standing at the door. 'Then why have you come here again?'

'No need to do anything for us. Just help them,' replied Kirti plainly, while pointing towards Hardial and his family.

'I can't help anyone. Just go away,' Manjit raised his voice and tried to close the door, but Gurkirat came forward and told him that he should listen to them once. Just once.

'Look at their faces *chacha ji*! Hardial just sold his kidney for the better future of his family. And he got nothing, but threats. You know very well that he won't be able to work properly now. Just think about their future,' said Gurkirat humbly.

Shabbily dressed Hardial and Meeto also came forward with folded hands. Two confused children stood silently by their side.

'I don't want to get involved in all this,' replied an adamant Manjit.

The students looked towards each other. Nobody said a word for a while. Tears rolled down Meeto's cheeks as she turned back, holding her children, but Hardial kept standing at his place with folded hands.

'A Sardar never denies help,' Gurkirat commented. 'They are the only ones who have the courage to sacrifice their lives for others. Our Gurus have also taught us to help the poor. If you won't help, you should rather not be a *sardar*.' This shook Manjit a bit, but he turned away and walked inside, leaving the door open.

Kirti, Rahul, Gurkirat and Hardial turned around to return. But Manjit had stopped after taking a few steps. He had seen his own younger version in Gurkirat, who possessed the same courage and determination. Hundreds of thoughts crossed his mind, but he was still in a dilemma.

'Wait!' Manjit shouted from inside and the group stopped to look back. 'I will help. But don't expect me to get directly involved anywhere.'

Rahul and Kirti smiled. Gurkirat was proud of his move. Manjit called them inside the living room. Gurkirat explained everything they had been through the entire last week. Kirti gave him a couple of leads she had got from the safe house and for the next few hours, they engaged in brainstorming.

'Now listen carefully,' Manjit told the students while Hardial and his wife listened, 'this doesn't look like a small racket to me. There is a hundred percent possibility of the involvement of influential people in it. So, whatever we do now onwards, should be done with a plan in place.'

'Got it!' Kirti and Rahul replied in unison while Gurkirat simply nodded.

'It was stupid of you to visit the hospital and safe house to get information openly, but then how would you know anyway,' Manjit said embarrassing the students. 'Such actions will only alert the perpetrators.'

'Would you mind preparing a cup of tea for me?' Manjit looked at Rahul and said, confusing him. Rahul gave a blank look. 'Would you?' Manjit asked, more serious this time and Rahul got up to do as directed.

'The first source of information is Jhakhar Hospital, but we cannot find anything there without the second source, the middlemen. The most important and vital information is housed in the authorisation committee's office,' Manjit continued.

'Why is the information of committee office most important?' Rahul asked from the kitchen.

'In 1994, the parliament enacted the Transplants of Human Organ Act 1994. It was a law banning the sale or purchase of organs and commercial transactions/dealings in the transplants of human organ(s). The law prohibited transplantation with organs from unrelated living donors and permitted family members. In only exceptional situations the Authorisation Committee constituted by the government could approve the organ donation outside family members. That too when the Authorisation Committee was satisfied that no financial transaction had taken place and donation was made only due to affection and charity. This law was enforced in Punjab in 1997,' Manjit enlightened everyone. Gurkirat secretly marvelled at Manjit's knowledge.

'But what does it have to do with Hardial's case?' Rahul enquired.

'Make sure the tea is good,' Manjit shouted without looking back and continued, 'Hardial has donated his kidney, but he has not given it to anyone in his family. And if he has given it to some other person, it must have been a special case for the authorisation committee to approve. They must have had to make sure that no monetary transaction was involved according to the law. But Hardial doesn't even know about the recipient. If he had signed papers like he says he did, what was written on them? We can only know from the committee's office. Once we find those documents, we can prove the involvement of people in this scam.'

'It is next to impossible to get access to the committee office!' Gurkirat exclaimed as Rahul came with a tray. Manjit threw an expressionless gaze at Rahul on seeing six cups in the tray. 'I had asked for me, not for everyone,' Manjit said as he lifted a cup. 'Bring me a packet of milk the next time we meet.'

Rahul kept the tray on the table as Kirti held back her laughter.

'Give me a day's time. I'll work on some plan,' Manjit said to Gurkirat. Everyone sipped tea from their cups, except Rahul. Manjit gestured him to pick up his cup saying, 'Don't worry. I'm giving you a waiver this time. You can have it.'

Kirti couldn't hold back her laughter anymore as an embarrassed Rahul slowly picked up his cup.

The students went to Manjit's house the next day after classes. He was ready with his plan. He directed Rahul to visit the blood bank, disguised as a poor labourer in dire need of money. The motive of sending Rahul there was to find Chandu and extract details about the modus operandi of the racket. Rahul's Bihari looks and dialect could aid in befriending Chandu, who was also a Bihari, as informed by Hardial.

To get information from the authorisation committee's office, Kirti volunteered. She told Manjit about Ratan Lal, the administrative officer, and how she always tricked him into doing things.

Gurkirat was assigned no special task. His duty was to simply keep an eye on Rahul and provide him backup since he was about to execute a risky task. As a last piece of advice before the trio got up to move, Manjit asked them to stay cautious and keep their eyes and ears open.

As the students left for the day's tasks, Manjit looked at the framed picture of his wife hung on the wall. 'I hope this doesn't turn out to be a bad decision,' he whispered.

The trio kicked off their journey to unearth one of the biggest scandals of human organ trade in the world.

***

Sticking to the plan, Rahul disguised himself as a poor man and went to Nathu's tea stall. He waited there for some time in anticipation that Chandu, whose description he had already taken from Hardial, might visit there. But he didn't. After waiting for a while, he went to the blood bank with Gurkirat trailing behind, keeping an eye on him. Rahul walked up to the front desk and spoke in a made-up Bihari accent. He offered to donate blood in return for some money. After actually donating one unit, he asserted that he needed money urgently and wanted to donate more. But the doctor, considering Rahul's skinny build, refused to take another one. Rahul implored him repeatedly to deliberately get himself noticed.

'But doctor! I am in dire need of money,' Rahul pleaded loudly. 'If you can't take more blood now, at least give me an advance of six months and I promise I will keep donating regularly.'

'We can't do that! It's a blood bank, not an actual bank,' the doctor said and asked him to leave.

Rahul did not budge until they called the security guards. His efforts to see Chandu did not prove fruitful. He sulked outside the blood bank and felt dizzy; all that drama had yielded nothing. When he was about to move, a person called him from behind. He was Chandu. Rahul could easily identify him. He hesitated at first, but then gathered enough confidence to face him.

'What bhaiya ji, why were you so loud inside?' Chandu asked while examining Rahul from head to toe. 'Why are you so troubled? You need money?'

'Yes,' Rahul replied.

'Then go find some work or a job. Biharis have a lot of options here in Punjab,' Chandu spoke in a typical Bihari accent.

'My employer has betrayed me. He had promised to give me twenty thousand rupees as advance for my sister's marriage. The ceremony is next week and I can't go back without money,' Rahul replied, trying to sound genuinely stressed. 'I don't know what to do now.' Standing at a distance, Gurkirat chuckled at Rahul's expressions, which he found funny.

'So that is the case,' Chandu said. 'What if I help you solve this problem?'

'You can't even imagine how much I will be thankful to you,' Rahul replied with his hands folded.

'No need to be thankful. Who will help us if we don't help our brothers in need,' said Chandu with a smile. 'And trust me, I can help you make a lot more than just twenty thousand.'

Rahul could clearly see Chandu trying to throw bait. Rahul looked like a potential donor to Chandu and he had already started to trap him.

'You will have to come with me,' Chandu said. Rahul thought for a while, thinking about the risk involved if he agreed to accompany Chandu, but he also knew that it could be the only chance to gather more information about the racket.

'Take me wherever you want, I just want money,' Rahul said, inducing a greedy smile on Chandu's face.

Chandu got his scooter from the parking and asked Rahul to hop on. Gurkirat had been watching all this from a distance. He kick-started his Kinetic Honda which belonged to Kirti. As expected, Chandu took Rahul to Jhakhar Hospital, and Gurkirat followed them.

Upon entering the hospital, Rahul was made to sit in the waiting area while Chandu went in search of Raju. In exactly ten minutes, Chandu and Raju came and started luring Rahul into selling his kidney. Rahul listened to everything carefully.

'Mahadev!' Rahul exclaimed, faking amazement. 'I will get five lakh rupees for a kidney?'

'You heard it right,' Chandu and Raju said in unison, thinking they had successfully lured Rahul.

'But bhaiya ji, are you sure that I will be alright after operation?' Rahul asked.

At this juncture, Raju stood up and repeated exactly what he had done in front of Hardial. He pulled up his shirt from behind and showed his own operation scar. Rahul then pretended that there was almost no worry in his mind, but said that he still wanted to meet the doctor for final assurance. Actually, Rahul simply wanted to see the doctor's face. Chandu and Raju took Rahul inside the doctor's cabin. The two doctors there convinced Rahul that there was no risk involved in donating a kidney.

Rahul had made a mental note of the names of the two doctors he met.

Raju was about to ask Rahul something when his phone rang. Raju moved a few steps away and took the call, but Rahul had his ears prying at the tele-conversation.

'Namaste Tinku bhai,' Raju said and started listening carefully to the person on the other end. After about a couple of minutes, he suddenly looked towards Rahul.

'Don't worry Tinku bhai! The work will be completed today itself,' he said while still looking at Rahul and disconnected the phone call. He walked towards Rahul and Chandu, and took Chandu aside to talk to him in private.

Raju had received a call from his boss Tinku, who had asked him to get a donor urgently. There was a recipient who was ready to spend double the amount to get a kidney, and luckily, Rahul's blood group matched. Both Chandu and Raju didn't want to let this opportunity go and planned to keep Rahul at the hospital till the removal of his kidney on that day itself.

'Fortune favours the vigilant,' Raju said to Rahul, smiling. 'You are lucky! My boss has just confirmed that a recipient is already available for your kidney.'

'Oh! Isn't that great?' Rahul said, nervously. 'So when do I have to undergo this operation?'

'Tomorrow,' answered Chandu.

Rahul was perplexed at this sudden, unplanned turn of events. He had never expected this. He looked here and there to catch the sight of Gurkirat, who was already sitting in the waiting area, secretly monitoring Rahul and his activities. Rahul tried to handle the situation himself. He told Chandu and Raju that he was not prepared, but Raju and Chandu refused to listen to him. When they suspected that Rahul was trying to back out, they tried playing another trick.

'Ummm... if you want some time to think, there is no problem. We will let you ponder over it, but some of the tests must be done today. Reports for these tests take time to come,' Raju said and called two ward boys. Before Rahul could speak anything, Raju instructed, 'Take this man to the lab for his tests.'

Rahul didn't get time to react. The ward boys took him to the lab and Rahul couldn't resist any more, from the fear of getting his cover blown. Chandu and Raju followed them. Gurkirat, who was watching everything, smelled something fishy. He also slunk behind them. Inside the lab, the doctor filled a syringe with a serum for Rahul, but since he was a medical student, Rahul understood that the doctor was trying to give him a sedative. He had to do something, and quickly. He pretended to feel an uncontrollable pressure in his bladder and told them that he wanted to urinate urgently.

The doctor asked one of the ward boys to take him to the washroom a few yards away, at the end of the corridor, outside the lab. Rahul went inside and the lab boy waited outside. It was time to act. Gurkirat, who had been waiting in one corner of the corridor, walked up to the ward boy and told him that the doctor had called him. The moment the ward boy went inside the lab, Gurkirat quickly entered the washroom, took Rahul, and both of them silently whisked away.

'Yes sir?' the ward boy said, looking at the doctor.

'Where is the patient?' the doctor asked.

'He is in the washroom. A sardaar ji told me you have called me,' the boy said.

'I did not call anyone. Go back and bring him inside!' the doctor said simply.

The ward boy went to the washroom, only to find Rahul missing. He came back running and informed everyone. Chandu and Raju ran towards the waiting area, but there was no sign of Rahul. They took their scooter and started looking for him around the hospital, but they could not trace him. It made them angry. A potential donor had ditched them. Raju informed Tinku, who suspected something fishy and asked him to remain alert.

Rahul and Gurkirat headed straight to Manjit Singh's residence. Rahul was panting. The whole episode had scared him. What if they had managed to remove his kidney forcibly, he thought. Sitting in the rear seat of the Kinetic, Rahul looked up at the sky and thanked god, as Gurkirat drove. Upon meeting Manjit, they informed him about what had happened.

'Good job,' Manjit complimented Rahul, his face still expressionless, 'but it would have been better if you had stayed there till morning. We would have got more evidence about the fake paperwork they do.'

'...And would have actually got my kidney removed,' Rahul mumbled and Gurkirat laughed.

'There's one thing I forgot to tell you. Raju spoke with someone named Tinku over a call and I think it was his boss,' Rahul said.

On hearing the name Tinku, there was a grimace on Manjit's forehead. It appeared as if the name sounded familiar to him.

***

While Rahul and Gurkirat were away finding information at Jhakhar Hospital, Kirti was carrying out her own investigation with the help of Ratan Lal, the administrative officer at Medical College, who also had the additional charge of managing documentation of the Authorisation Committee's office. A copy of certain files, if not all, related to kidney donors and recipients had to be there in his office, Kirti believed.

Ratan Lal used to have lunch in his in-campus accommodation and Kirti knew it well. She thought of a plan. Kirti called him on his office's telephone number from the PCO outside Medical College just moments before lunch time was about to begin.

'Hello sir, Kirti this side,' she said politely.

'Hello my dear Kirti. What makes you call me?' he replied with a broad smile on his face, as if Kirti could see it.

'Sir, how long are you going to be in office? I have some urgent work with you,' Kirti said, knowing well that Ratan Lal had to leave for home in a few minutes.

'Dear, I am just leaving for lunch! It will take me half an hour. We can meet afterwards and have a cup of tea together,' Ratan took the opportunity and asked Kirti.

'Oh! But sir, I have already come out of my home. It will hardly take ten minutes for me to reach your office,' pleaded Kirti.

'There is no fun in meeting in a hurry, dear. Let it be after lunch,' replied Ratan Lal in an overly sweet tone.

'Sir, can I at least wait for you in your office till you get back from?' Kirti acted according to her plan. She knew Ratan would not deny.

'Yes yes, why not!' I will ask my orderly to keep the office unlocked for you. I will go and get back quickly. You see, diabetic people can't skip lunch, he he...' Ratan Lal said. Before he could say goodbye, Kirti disconnected the call. Her job was done.

Kirti entered the college premises and waited for Ratan Lal to go to his accommodation. When he entered his room, she immediately walked to his office. The orderly let her sit in Ratan's office. Kirti sat there for a couple of minutes silently, and then with the help of her peripheral vision to keep an eye at the door, she started looking for files when the orderly went outside.

There was one big cupboard which housed all the files Ratan Lal was responsible for. Luckily, it was open. She started searching for the stack of files related to organ donation. As anticipated, she found the stack and let out a sigh of relief. The next task was to look for the file with Hardial's name. Time was slipping away. She quickly shuffled through the files. There were four rows of the concerned stack. She had searched to the third row when she heard approaching footsteps. She quickly yet silently shut the cupboard close and seated herself on the chair. It was the orderly who had come with a glass of water for Kirti. The moment he left after Kirti took the glass, she approached the cupboard again and began searching the fourth row, but sadly she didn't find any file pertaining to Hardial Singh. Little did she know that Hardial's name was changed when the file was presented before the authorisation committee.

She wiped the sweat off her forehead and walked out of the office. She told the orderly that she had some urgent work and she would come back to meet Ratan Lal. She headed straight towards Manjit Singh's house, where Rahul and Gurkirat were already waiting for her. She narrated everything and felt disappointed for not being able to get any information. Her friends, however, lauded her effort and bravery. The information that students had gathered till that time was still very less, but for Manjit Singh, an experienced lawyer, it was enough to prepare an interim affidavit on behalf of Hardial Singh.

'Take Hardial along with you tomorrow and submit this affidavit in the SSP's[2] office,' Manjit handed over a typed piece of paper to Gurkirat and said firmly.

---

2 Senior Superintendent of Police

'But, chacha ji, Hardial had already submitted one complaint, and nothing had happened,' Gurkirat said.

'Hardial went to the police station of his area and talked to some munshi there, who was just ignorant or disinterested. But this affidavit will be submitted straightaway in the SSP's office. Police will be bound to act on this one,' Manjit said.

'And what about Hardial's safety? And his family's?' Kirti asked.

'We have to ask him to shift to a safer place till he gets justice,' replied Manjit. 'Remember, we are going to put our hands in a beehive.' There was a deathly silence in the room.

The trio took Hardial to the SSP's office the next day. The first document to unearth the infamous kidney scandal was submitted in May 2000. The affidavit was then marked to SP[3] City by SSP, who then further marked it to DSP for legal action. The SHO[4], on getting the orders, launched the investigation. The first FIR in this case, No. 116, was registered by a fearless and honest trainee IPS officer - Partap Singh, ACP[5] - on 30 May 2000.

Hardial shifted to his friend Nathu's house and Partap Singh also detailed two guards for his personal security. A trainee at the time, Partap didn't even hesitate to include names of high-profile people involved in the so-called scam. Things went as planned and when everyone thought that justice was about to be delivered, Partap got orders for his posting out of Amritsar, that too a week before his training was supposed to conclude.

---

3 Superintendent of Police

4 Station House Officer

5 Assistant Commissioner of Police

Chapter 4

SHO of B division police station, Sanjay Beri, was made the investigating officer of the case after Partap left. Acting upon the FIR as originally written by the trainee Partap Singh, he conducted a series of raids at various places in Amritsar and nabbed four culprits. Higher authorities lauded the achievements of his team. The SHO, who wanted to depict himself as a hero, asked for a permission to hold a press conference in this regard, but was promptly denied. The challan was submitted in court and finally the culprits were sent to jail. The case was closed.

Manjit came to know about this from one of his sources in the police department. He was curious if the middlemen had been caught. To validate the authenticity of the raids by the SHO, he made a plan with the help of his source where he could visit the police station along with Hardial to identify the arrested culprits. Manjit asked Gurkirat to bring Hardial to his house that evening. Gurkirat did as asked after his college was over for the day.

Upon reaching the police station with Manjit and Gurkirat, Manjit's source took Hardial inside the police station. When questioned by the SHO, he introduced Hardial as a plumber who had come to check the leakage inside the cells. Upon getting a closer look at the convicts, Hardial was left baffled.

Hardial came out and told Manjit that they were no culprits. The arrested people were in fact poor donors like him, who were captured from safe houses, but later shown to have been arrested from Company Gardens. Hardial had recognized two of them who were there with him in the safe house.

Manjit had an inkling that something like this would happen. Police's actions had left the students heartbroken. All their hard work and dedication for nothing!

'We should go to the SSP again,' Rahul said, frustrated. 'And tell him about the actual culprits.'

'You can't!' replied Manjit, sipping his evening tea at his house the next day after the visit to the police station. 'We had already submitted the affidavit in his office and despite his orders, the case was never handled by an experienced officer, but a trainee, Partap Singh. And the case was shut hurriedly. This only means that there is some pressure on them – whether from inside or outside, I am not sure. But there is something wrong for sure. My source also told me that Partap's original FIR was not followed and his training was cut short. He was forcibly sent back.'

Manjit's words depressed the students even more. This could only mean that this kidney scam was rooted deeper than they knew.

'This scam is murkier than we thought!' Gurkirat exclaimed plainly, unknowingly scratching his thick beard.

'I still wonder who included the names of the donors in the FIR?' Kirti spoke. 'If the SHO has acted according to the FIR, then we should not forget that the FIR was originally registered by Partap.'

'Are you suspecting him?' asked Rahul.

'The facts are forcing me to suspect him, Rahul!' replied Kirti.

'Then why was the charge taken back from him? Why was he sent back before the completion of his training period?' Rahul hurled these questions in one go.

'Maybe because he completed his task before time and the others wanted to take some of the credit too,' replied Kirti.

'If somehow the Police department is protecting the real culprits, we cannot deny Partap's role in it,' said Manjit.

The four of them shared confused and depressed looks.

'Let us not lose hope and keep collecting proofs, only this time we need to think a step ahead,' said Manjit, breaking the silence. 'This time we will go to the media.'

'I have a cousin who is a press correspondent. We can trust him,' Gurkirat said at once upon hearing Manjit.

'That's a good idea! Then the media will build pressure on the police to take necessary action,' replied Kirti, quite cheerfully.

'Why are you thinking about the future? Why can't we go to the media right now? We have a copy of Hardial's affidavit.' Rahul's doubt was a genuine one.

'Because then the Police will assure the media that they have already taken action in this regard. They will also prove that the convicts were involved in kidney trade. Neither do we have any proof that those who got caught are only kidney donors, nor we do have any evidence that they were not involved in the organ trade,' explained Manjit. 'That's the reason we need to have enough information to prove our points to the media. Our arsenal is empty; we need more ammunition.'

The four of them gathered in that room knew that even if one of them wanted to back out at this point, the others wouldn't let it happen. After all, with knowledge comes moral responsibility that arises out of that knowledge, and these four could feel the weight of their responsibility now. They probably knew more about this newfound kidney scam than anyone else. If this pursuit died here, nobody would come to know about it. Moreover, a lot of others would be wronged by then, and a lot more palms would have been greased.

These students were aspiring doctors of tomorrow and something like this had only strengthened their resolve to get to the bottom and uproot a scam which was tarnishing the image of their future profession. Talking about Manjit, he was at it only because he could see in these students his younger self. If only, he had found a 'Manjit' to guide him back then.

***

Raju informed Chandu over a phonecall, about an urgent meeting called by their boss. The two went to Sohan International Hotel, a famous one in Amritsar at that time, and waited for their boss Tinku, who arrived an hour late in his white Mercedes W210 E-class. A man with short build in his late forties, he looked much older. Tinku was always seen dressed in suits, especially white ones. His protruding belly and dark, uneven skin tone never came in the way of his style statement.

Chandu and Raju bent to touch their boss' feet. Tinku dramatically blessed them both at once by running his hands over each one's head and then gestured them to follow him inside the hotel's restaurant. Tinku started the conversation by appreciating the duo's contribution in business and then informed them about the FIR that was registered and the subsequent action taken by Police. When Tinku's words worried the two, he assured them that nothing more would happen as the case was now closed, because of his *connections*.

'The police have successfully cracked the case and nabbed the culprits!' Tinku said with a sarcastic smile. 'Now there is no kidney trade going on in Amritsar.' Tinku then laughed for a while as the other two stared blankly at him, too slow to understand his sarcasm.

'Now listen to me carefully!' Tinku had laughed his heart out by now. He poured himself warm milk from the kettle brought in by a waitress, took some almonds out of his coat's pocket and put them in the milk before continuing, 'It is the right time to expand our business and that's the reason I have called you here. I want you to visit all the cities of Punjab and make contacts. I am also in touch with some contacts of other countries and soon things will materialise. Then you both will have to work very hard. With the Kidney racket busted as per police records, it's time for us to go global now.'

'No issues Tinku bhaiya! We are always with you,' replied an excited Raju.

'I am proud of you both! Plan your visits and keep me informed,' Tinku said and got up to leave. 'Eat anything you want here and don't pay the bill!'

***

Gurkirat and Rahul thought of keeping an eye on the safe house for a couple of days. A doctor, who was a regular visitor there, caught their attention. He would enter the safe house every morning at nine and leave in the afternoon.

Rahul and Gurkirat followed him one day and found his address and name. When they came to a solid conclusion that he was employed to look after the donors, they thought of a plan to enter the house. Next day, about fifteen minutes after the doctor went out of the safe house in the afternoon, Gurkirat, who was ready wearing his white coat, approached one of the gates.

'Open the door, I am Dr Gurkirat! Dr Aman had asked me to administer these injections to the patients inside,' Gurkirat said confidently to one of the security guards. The guard hesitated to open the gate initially, but when Gurkirat told him that it was a serious health matter, he let Gurkirat in. When he entered the house, Rahul took cover nearby and kept an eye on the doctor, in case he returned.

The security guard guided Gurkirat to the room where the donors were kept. When he entered inside, he was petrified to see the condition of that unhygienic place. There was only one fan in a 700 square feet room of ten beds. Five weak and half-conscious patients were lying on five beds. They were surprised to see the new doctor in that place. Gurkirat sensed their apprehension and assured them that he was there to help them. They did not believe him at all! It took some time for Gurkirat to calm them and win their trust. He then quickly asked them their names and addresses. He wrote every detail about the patients in his small diary.

'They must have taken all of you in front of some committee. Do you remember what happened there?' Gurkirat asked quickly.

All of them agreed that they were taken in front of some

persons for verification, but they spoke nothing there as the procedure took hardly two minutes.

'Please think harder! Try to recall if anything specific happened there,' Gurkirat emphasised, but no one remembered anything in detail.

Gurkirat looked towards his watch. He had already spent twenty odd minutes there. He wanted to get out as soon as possible, before the security guards could suspect him. Without worthwhile details, a saddened Gurkirat walked towards the door.

'Wait, I think I remember something,' one of the patients said.

Gurkirat stopped, turned around and went towards the patient's bed.

'One of the persons called me Rohit Yadav and the others quickly gestured him to keep shut,' he said. 'I thought he was mistaken, because my original name is Rudra Prasad.'

'Anything more that you can recall?' Gurkirat asked anxiously while jotting down the name.

'That's it, that is the only thing I found strange,' said the patient.

Gurkirat then quickly left the room and in no time, was outside the safe house. He had got names and addresses of donors and an additional name he could further investigate – Rohit Yadav.

***

A get-together was planned at Manjit's house the same day after college hours. Kirti would often remain out of her house with the excuse that extra anatomy classes were scheduled and she was attending them regularly. Rahul and Gurkirat had time till 8:30 p.m. before the warden would start his round around the hostel. The three would use this time to work on their investigation.

'Rohit Yadav,' Manjit said thoughtfully, 'the name holds the mystery. We may get answers if we get to know who he is.'

'I think we shouldn't be focusing on this. It could simply be a mistake,' Rahul suggested.

'It could be,' Gurkirat said, 'but that patient said that he remembered others asking the person to keep shut.'

'What if we go after it and it turns out to be a dead end?' Kirti said.

'We won't find out until we find out,' said Gurkirat.

'Now what is your plan?' asked Manjit.

'Rahul and I will look for a suitable opportunity to search Ratan Lal's office in the middle of the night,' replied Gurkirat. 'His office is close to our hostel's rear exit.'

The others were stunned by this statement coming from Gurkirat, who was otherwise a sucker for law and order, and discipline.

'Look, Kirti has tried once already and we cannot put her in danger. It's our turn now,' said Gurkirat.

'Go ahead! But be careful,' Manjit said, without looking at them.

***

Chandu and Raju embarked on their mission as updated by Tinku and took off to Jalandhar and Ludhiana to establish their contacts. A number of people and hospitals agreed to work with them. A meeting of the newly-added middlemen was fixed with Tinku, who explained their role to them in detail. To expand their business, they were told to visit all the dialysis centres and contact patients in need.

Middlemen soon started meeting patients and offered them deals according to their financial status. Transplants also began in Jalandhar and Ludhiana in full swing. But the increased demand of kidneys required more donors, so the middlemen started luring poor people openly in such cities. The demand went up to such an extent within few days that the middlemen failed to produce enough kidney donors.

Pressure on the middlemen goons built up to such an extent that when they could not find anyone, they picked up people forcibly at gunpoint and began to remove their kidneys against their will. Cheaper availability of kidneys in Amritsar caught the attention of some recipients of other states as well, and soon, they also started contacting these middlemen from Punjab.

Everyone involved, whether it was a middleman, doctor or advocate, minted money, except the poor donor who couldn't even raise his voice after the wrong had been done. With India enjoying accelerated growth in GDP in the beginning of the new millennium, people were not hesitating to spend lakhs of rupees on their health, especially kidney patients. Tinku was elated with the speedy work Chandu and Raju were putting in. He called them up for a meeting one day.

October 2000. Amritsar

'What a fine day to eat *poori chhole* and discuss business!' Tinku said as the three of them sat on a table outside *Kanha*

Sweets in the afternoon sun. As usual, Tinku was dressed in white, but not in a way that would make a fashion statement. His tight trousers were about to tear apart from the seams and his white sweater with blue stripes failed to cover his dark-skinned belly flab, which peeped from below the torso.

'So, partners, what will you drink? Lassi or tea?' Tinku asked. What surprised Raju and Chandu was not Tinku's counterfeited politeness, but the fact that he had called them *partners*.

'Partners?' stammered Raju.

'Yes! Partners!' Tinku spoke, 'From today onwards, you are partners - like me - in this business. Big boss is very happy with your performance and he has asked me to raise your stakes to a permanent share of 5% in the whole business.'

Chandu and Raju looked at each other in awe. Until that day, they hadn't heard of any big boss. They used to regard Tinku as their only boss, who they thought was directly in touch with Jhakhar Hospital. They felt out of the world in that moment because of getting such recognition.

'We are really thankful to big boss. But who exactly is he? Can we meet him?' asked a curious Chandu.

'Ricky Bhatia,' said Tinku as he gulped a large bite of poori, 'and it's not so easy to meet him. You've just gained a position in business. Work harder to maintain it and earn your chance to meet him.'

'We will continue giving our best, bhaiya ji,' replied Raju.

'I'm giving you more responsibility now. Since my focus will be on international clients now, you handle the local ones I used to handle,' said Tinku as he gently and dramatically wiped his mouth with his shining white handkerchief.

Tinku and his boss, the local kingpin, Ricky Bhatia wanted to expand the kidney business beyond Indian borders. Work had already begun in that direction. Money in pounds was worth more than money in rupees. And they had already managed to establish their contacts in the UK, New Zealand and Nepal. Kidney patients in those countries, when contacted, agreed to visit India for their transplant.

***

Medical College had a shift of ten security guards for night patrolling along the perimeter as well as for guarding the front and rear gates. Four of them guarded the gates and one guard roamed around the campus perimeter. It was his job to check and confirm locks at all the offices, classrooms and labs after the students and staff left the campus. Rahul and Gurkirat watched the activity of the patrolling guard for a couple of days and then thought of a plan. But for the plan to work, it was imperative for Rahul to befriend the campus security guard chief, who was a hard nut to crack.

Rahul complained of never being given an easier task, but Gurkirat pacified him with the promise of homemade *saag*. Motivated by the promise of food, Rahul found out the weakness of the security guard through his watchfulness.

Ramcharan, an ex-army soldier, could smell a bottle of scotch from miles away and was drawn to it like a moth drawn to lamps. Therefore, Rahul and Gurkirat spent a major chunk of their monthly allowance on a premium whiskey and gave it to Ramcharan, citing the reason as Gurkirat's birthday. Reluctant at first, Ramcharan finally succumbed to the weight of a 750ml sealed bottle, but cautioned Rahul and Gurkirat to go back to the hostel as it was past hostel-curfew time. A couple of days later, Rahul again went to him with another bottle, though with a different reason. It took one more bottle and a period of almost a month for Rahul to finally befriend the security guard.

'Why not execute our plan tonight?' asked Gurkirat.

'Ramcharan is in the zone, so I guess the sooner the better,' Rahul replied.

'Great! Be prepared to get boozed today then,' said Gurkirat with a witty smile.

'What? I will have to drink with him? You know I'm a teetotaller,' replied Rahul.

'The plan is to engage him for a while. And it would be best if you booze him up,' said Gurkirat. 'Plus, you don't drink, but you can act well, I know. Remember when you almost lost your kidney that day? Superb acting!'

'Why always me?' replied Rahul, but then he agreed.

At around ten in the night, both Rahul and Gurkirat walked up to Ramcharan's picquet alongside the main gate. Gurkirat stopped in the dark a few metres away and hid himself.

'Ram Ram fauji bhai,' greeted Rahul, desperately trying to hide his anxiety for the task at hand.

'What have you brought today, doctor saab,' asked Ramcharan as he rolled his long handlebar moustache.

'Today I'm feeling homesick, fauji bhai. So, I wanted to feel better,' Rahul pulled out a quarter of whiskey and continued. 'I have come to you with this bottle. Only you can be my company.'

'It's so nice of you, but I can't drink with you. You're a student, and drinking within campus for you is an offence.

Moreover, I avoid drinking on Thursdays,' the guard replied.

Rahul, who was unprepared for this answer, went dumb for a minute. He did not know what to say, but didn't want to let go of the opportunity. They had delayed their plan too much already.

'Every day is god's day, then why differentiate? And you drinking from bottles I've been giving you is okay, but one small peg for me and with me is an offence?' Rahul said and put two disposable glasses on the bench. 'I have always liked our veteran soldiers and that's why I've been wanting to be friends with you, so that you can tell me stories from the field.'

'Today I can't, we can sit tomorrow,' Ramcharan didn't budge.

'Look, if you don't drink today, I will forget that we are friends. After all, a friend in need is...' Rahul said firmly.

'...a friend indeed,' Ramcharan at once took the glass that Rahul had just filled with whiskey, thinking that he might lose all future bottles from Rahul if he denied drinking that night.

Rahul immediately filled the glasses with club soda. Ramcharan lifted the glass and looked towards Rahul, who seemed reluctant to drink, but knowing that Ramcharan's gaze was fixed on Rahul, he gulped the glass in one go. Ramcharan could see Rahul's facial muscles twitching as Rahul held back his gag reflex. Rahul then managed to smile at Ramcharan who gulped his whiskey too.

Poor Rahul had just lost his liquor virginity.

While the guard sat with Rahul, Gurkirat sneaked into the picquet and quickly searched for the keys for Ratan Lal's office. It's the one with an Amitabh Bachchan keychain, Kirti had already told Gurkirat. So it wasn't too hard to locate.

He then strode towards the main campus and broke into Ratan Lal's office. Carefully, he unlocked the cupboard described by Kirti and started searching for files of kidney donors. Row by row, he sifted through each file carefully. Despite his thorough scanning, he didn't find any file with the names of donors he had met at the safe house.

Gurkirat thought for a second, that all their efforts had gone in vain. He pulled a chair and seated himself, thinking about the case. Suddenly, the name 'Rohit Yadav' streamed into his mind and he jumped off the chair to resume his file-search.

His intuition led him to find a file marked as 'Rohit Yadav'. He was flabbergasted to see the details inside. There were affidavits inside the file, which bore the passport size photograph of Rudra Prasad, but the name had been changed to Rohit Yadav. Without any further ado, he took the file and carefully shut the cupboard. After locking the office and keeping the key back in the bunch inside the picquet, Gurkirat gestured continuously towards a half-conscious Rahul, who had boozed for the first time in his life. Ramcharan had already knocked off and was snoring on the bench with his head drooped to his chest.

Rahul took some time to understand that the task had been completed. Gurkirat had to almost carry Rahul back to their hostel room. He then stayed awake for the rest of the night, tending to Rahul, who vomited after every few minutes, before sleep took the better of him.

While a hung-over Rahul missed the classes the next day, Gurkirat and Kirti bunked them to go and meet Manjit at his residence.

'These are the proofs we needed!' Manjit exclaimed.

'These documents prove that Rudra Prasad was shown as Rohit Yadav to fool the authorisation committee. Fake ID and affidavits were prepared by lawyers and the same even got attested by the magistrate! A lot of people are involved here,' Manjit concluded.

'But why would they change the donor's name?' asked Kirti.

'To show him in relation with the kidney recipient, otherwise the donation is not possible according to the law,' Manjit answered. 'They showed Rohit, I mean Rudra, as the servant of recipient, who has been staying in their house since the last twenty years and regarded the recipient as his father.'

'God! So, they fool the authorisation committee in this way. They must have changed Hardial's name also. That's why I didn't find his file that day,' said Kirti.

The discovery of Rudra's file was a very strong link that could lead the students to prove the modus operandi of the kidney scandal.

'Now I can make a report with these documents attached. We will give it to the media. If it turns out as planned, there will be a lot of pressure on the police to go after the actual culprits,' Manjit said.

When the trio left, Manjit started working on the findings. He carefully examined each detail mentioned in the file. This time, they didn't have any scope of a miss or an error. He burnt midnight oil to prepare the report. Finally, when everything was almost ready in the wee hours of the morning, a group of men barged into his house and a helpless and struggling Manjit was taken against his will.

Chapter 5

It was almost dawn when two people sneaked inside Kirti's room. The bedroom door was open and this ambitious MBBS student, who had been up all-night, studying, was in deep sleep. Silhouette of two human figures with something in their hand inched forward towards her bed.

'Happy Birthday!' they shouted loudly, waking Kirti up in shock. At that very moment, one of them switched on the lights. It took a while for Kirti to catch her breath and then she got out of her bed to hug her father and mother. She was their only child.

'Mr Sharma, Mom had told me that you won't be able to come this time?' Kirti asked her father.

'She was right! I had some important work, but I finished it before time and got my leave sanctioned. Besides, NHPC[6] knew your birthday was approaching and they didn't want to mess with you,' her father replied. An engineer by profession, Abhilash Sharma was frequently transferred to various cities, but due to Kirti's education, he had decided not to take his family along and kept the mother and daughter at his parental house in Amritsar.

'You made my day, Papa!' exclaimed a happy Kirti.

---

6 National Hydro Electric Power Corporation

'And what about me?' asked her mother, Mrs Pragya Sharma.

'Well, you make my every day!' said Kirti and the trio hugged again.

They cut the cake together and chatted for a long time before crashing off to sleep again. At about 9 a.m., Kirti was woken up by the alarm. She just half-followed her morning routine and got ready in minutes. She was already late for college.

'Is there something important today,' her father asked while sipping his morning tea.

'Yes Papa! There is a guest lecture by Dr Bhasin at our college at 9:30 a.m.,' replied Kirti, rolling a parantha from the casserole, to eat on the way.

'That famous kidney surgeon?' asked her father.

'Yes! the same… he's a role model,' replied Kirti excitedly.

'Then there's no point asking you to take the day off today,' mumbled her father almost inaudibly.

Dr Pawan Bhasin was the alumnus of Holy City Medical College and a well-known kidney surgeon. He had been invited by the college for an expert talk with budding doctors on the topic 'Kidney Ailments'. His framed photograph along with a brief on his achievements was hung on the hall-of-fame wall inside their college premises. Many admired him, while some envied his fame. Kirti belonged to the former.

She reached college five minutes prior to the lecture, earliest that she had ever been for any class. She straightway headed to the seminar hall where students had already started to take their seats. Rahul and Gurkirat had reserved a seat for her, right in the center, on Rahul's request. He had also kept a bouquet of pink roses; red ones would have given away too much of his feelings. Gurkirat, as always, cringed at the way Rahul gave her the roses when she approached, stating it was from both of them. When Kirti hugged him in return, Rahul smiled so wide, he would have split at ears. And for a moment, he didn't even move, sat like a stunned statue. Kirti knew the roses were from one person only.

'One of the best birthdays I have had,' said Kirti as she adjusted herself in the seat, took out a notebook and a pen, all set for the lecture.

'Thank you,' replied an overwhelmed Rahul. 'It's because of the lecture by Dr Bhasin,' Gurkirat said and Kirti nodded, leaving Rahul dumb-faced.

The whole crowd started cheering and everyone stood up with an applause when Dr Bhasin entered the seminar hall from behind the stage's curtains, accompanied by Principal Dr Puneet Gupta. Six feet tall, quite a giant in front of a five-feet-four-inches tall principal, fair skinned and sporting a goatee, Dr Bhasin waved towards the students with a smile. Kirti was overjoyed to see him. Rahul was obviously envious of the half-bald doc. The clapping did not stop till all the guests were seated on the stage, with Dr Bhasin in the middle.

Dr Bhasin started his lecture after the principal's formal welcome and introductory speech. He spoke for about one hour and there was pin drop silence in the hall. After the lecture concluded, a round of applause rang through the college premises. Kirti was left hypnotised by the lecture. Dr Bhasin walked off the stage, waving at the applauding students. He was then escorted by the college authorities towards the exit.

'What a man!' said Kirti. 'And that's how you deliver a lecture.' Then, as an afterthought, she added, 'Guys! I want to meet him. I can't let this opportunity go.'

Rahul rolled his eyes in visible envy, even as Gurkirat grinned at Kirti's stupid request.

'It's not a fangirl thing,' Kirti retorted. 'It is about the kidney Scam. Let's see if this guy can help.'

'But how is that even possible?' Gurkirat asked.

'I know just the way. Follow me!' replied Kirti as she walked out of the hall towards the principal's office.

Ratan Lal was in-charge of refreshments that day. He stood outside the principal's office, where Dr Bhasin and his associates were served tea. Kirti convinced Ratan Lal and he requested Dr Bhasin, who had come out for a phone call, to meet the students for an autograph. The surgeon couldn't say no to Ratan Lal and asked him to send the students inside the office. The principal was surprised to see the trio.

'Go on, say it!' Dr Bhasin humbly asked Kirti, who was struggling to speak in his presence.

'Sir, you are an inspiration for us. We just wanted to have your autograph,' replied Kirti and forwarded her notebooks towards Dr Bhasin.

'Sir, do you know...' Kirti said out of nowhere in a deep voice, while Dr Bhasin was scribbling on her notebook, 'there is a kidney racket going on in the city.'

Gurkirat and Rahul were taken aback and exchanged befuddled looks at Kirti's behaviour. They did not understand what Kirti was up to. She had not discussed anything like this with them. The principal batted an eye and asked her to leave, but she didn't care. Dr Bhasin's pen had stopped scribbling and he seemed surprised at Kirti's awkward behaviour. She continued rattling out information without a pause as a confused Dr Bhasin listened.

'Enough!' the principal barged in. Dr Bhasin raised his hand towards the principal, gesturing him to remain silent. 'You must be mistaken. I'm quite sure nothing like this is feasible. If it had been there, I would have known. After all, I too am a nephrologist,' Dr Bhasin said while adjusting his oval shaped spectacles.

'If you believe me sir, I can show you evidences,' said Kirti.

'If you have any evidence, bring it to me. I will not leave any stone unturned to catch the culprits. They are maligning our noble profession; they must be brought to justice,' replied Dr Bhasin while staring at Kirti.

'We will soon provide you with the details. Thank you, sir,' thinking she had struck the right chord, a hopeful Kirti thanked Dr Bhasin and the trio walked out of the principal's office.

'What was that, Kirti?' Gurkirat retorted in his usual heavy voice. 'You should have at least discussed it with us before pulling that card. How could we trust him?'

'It was not planned. I just couldn't control myself when I met him,' replied the ever-daring and carefree Kirti. 'But I know he is a gem of a person and he will surely help us. Besides, we have already touched rock bottom and there's nothing to lose now.'

'If you say so,' Rahul, latently impressed with Kirti's act, mumbled as the trio walked out of the college building towards the exit gate.

'Forget about this now! It's time for my birthday party,' Kirti tried cheering her friends, Gurkirat most of all. Rahul hardly needed any cheering up in her company anyway.

'It better not be a bakery this time.' Gurkirat commented, teasingly.

'I'm taking you two for fine dining,' replied Kirti, inducing a glow in the eyes of her hosteler friends.

The food at the restaurant was quite costly, but Kirti didn't care that day. She was on a different kind of high. Gurkirat and Rahul also didn't bother ordering the specials for the day. Regular, tasteless, hostel food had corroded their taste buds and it was time to bring them back to work. Kirti laughed at Rahul hogging like animals.

'Anything else for you bulls?' Kirti asked, insulting playfully.

'Dessert please!' Gurkirat answered so casually that Rahul let out a sputtering burst.

Kirti threw a rolled napkin at Rahul and called for the waiter anyway.

'We should come here more often. The food is amazing. Thank you for this wonderful treat, Kirti,' Gurkirat said and burped twice in between the lines.

'I second Guri,' Rahul said with an even louder burp.

'If only you two try to be more civilized,' Kirti commented while nodding her head, gesturing the two to look at nearby tables, for the audience their burps had gathered. 'Now get up! We still have lectures to attend.' Oblivious of things unfolding at the other end, the three friends enjoyed the calm for a while before the storm.

The trio reached the campus where the lecture post lunch was about to begin. In the middle of the last lecture of that day, the peon entered the classroom and handed over a piece of paper to the teacher. After reading it, the teacher looked towards Kirti, Rahul and Gurkirat. He called them to the front and told them to leave the class immediately as the college had suspended them for a month. Gurkirat asked the reason, but nothing was mentioned on the order, except undisciplined conduct. They took that piece of paper and went straight towards the principal's office to seek clarification, but they were not allowed to meet him.

'What is our fault?' Kirti asked, waving the paper in front of Rahul and Gurkirat.

'We don't know,' replied Rahul and Gurkirat.

Kirti walked into Ratan Lal's office, but was left disappointed when even he could not justify the reason for their suspension. He only said, 'Must be your fangirl moment with Dr Bhasin that upset the principal.'

'This surely has something to do with us meeting Dr Bhasin,' Gurkirat said outside Ratan Lal's office. 'But it's certainly not because we trespassed the principal's privacy.'

'I have a feeling Guri is right,' Rahul added.

Kirti remained silent and kept walking.

'And the principal is not even ready to listen to us,' Kirti said after a while.

'Indiscipline!' Rahul scoffed, 'how specific.'

'I think we stirred something we shouldn't have,' Gurkirat said. 'It's either the principal or Dr Bhasin.'

As much as Kirti wanted to shut Gurkirat up for linking this to her idol Dr Bhasin, she couldn't ignore, considering this as one grim possibility.

'Only Manjit chachaji can help us,' Gurkirat suggested and the trio agreed. Without delay, the three hired a rickshaw from outside college and left.

'He is not home,' said Rahul. They had been ringing the doorbell for a while now.

'Let us wait outside then,' Kirti said in a pale voice, opposite to how she had sounded at the start of the day. The three sat on the footpath opposite Manjit's house. They waited for almost two hours, but there was still no sign of Manjit. It soon began to get dark.

'Papa must be waiting for me,' Kirti said while looking at the watch. 'I must go home. We can meet Manjit bhaiya tomorrow.'

'Yes! You must leave. It's your birthday,' replied Rahul.

Right when Kirti got up to leave, Gurkirat noticed something unusual as darkness crept.

'Look!' he pointed towards Manjit's house. 'All the lights inside the house are switched on. Manjit chachaji is at home. Or maybe someone else is!'

Gurkirat hammered the doorbell button for a few times, but to no avail. When the doorbell was not answered, he banged his fist at the front door. To everyone's surprise, it swung open with force.

Alarmed, the students ran inside. What worried them more was that the doors inside were also open. They searched for Manjit from one room to another, but there was no clue of him. When they entered his office, they saw that someone has rummaged around inside his office.

'Please Waheguru,' Gurkirat mumbled as his eyes widened, as if some realization had dawned upon him in that moment and he knew exactly what he had to look for. 'It better not be,' he said and searched through the pile of files on the table to find the one he was looking for – the file containing all evidences and findings so far. And to his disappointment, it was empty. Just what he had feared.

'All evidences are gone,' he said as he stood there, petrified.

'We should not have trusted him,' said Rahul.

'Shut up you fool! Do not jump to conclusions,' Kirti retorted. 'If he had to do this, why did he prepare Hardial's affidavit in the first place? Why did he keep guiding us so far? And look at this mess. I think something is gravely wrong.'

The trio went out of the house to enquire from other houses in Manjit's locality. They were surprised and disappointed to know that no one had seen Manjit since the last two days. Scared and panicked, Kirti, Rahul and Gurkirat didn't know what to do.

'We must go to the police and file a missing person complaint,' Rahul suggested and others agreed.

Kirti insisted to tag along, but she was sent home by Gurkirat. Rahul and Gurkirat went to the local police station and tried to register a complaint, but the SHO ignored them, stating that they were in no way related to the person whose complaint was being filed. He rather suspected them. It was the ID cards of Rahul and Gurkirat that saved them that day. Tired and depressed, Gurkirat and Rahul went back to the hostel and called Kirti.

'Is there something wrong?' Kirti's father asked as she hung up the phone with a grim face.

'No! Nothing Papa,' she replied. Even though he knew she was keeping something from him, he took her to the dinner table saying, 'Don't worry, all will be well.'

Though her mind was still stuck in the day's events, Kirti pretended to be happy in front of her parents. Gurkirat and Rahul spent another sleepless night in the hostel.

Chirping birds woke Kirti up early the next morning and she went downstairs. Her father was getting ready to leave. While he savoured paranthas in the breakfast, Kirti helped keep his luggage outside. She usually dropped him at the bus stand on her Kinetic Honda. Owing to her driving skills, Mr Sharma managed to catch his bus in time. As Kirti turned back to go to the college, a black Mahindra Jeep started following her. She noticed it in the rear-view mirror. There were two men inside. They kept trailing her and when she reached closer to the college, they nudged her Kinetic with one corner of the jeep. Kirti fell, but sustained no injury, save a couple of bruises. The jeans she wore were slightly torn from the knees due to the impact. She quickly got up and looked back at the men inside angrily. She could only see the eyes; the rest of the faces were covered with a muffler. There was no number plate on the jeep and the engine kept on running.

'Hey, you assholes! I know it was intentional,' Kirti yelled at them, but there was no reaction.

Suddenly, the driver shifted the gear and the car came forward towards Kirti. It stopped a few metres away. She was frightened, but stood still, staring hard into the driver's eyes. Before Kirti could react again, the jeep turned back and within seconds, was out of her sight.

'Clearly, someone is trying to intimidate me,' she thought to herself.

Pulling herself back together, she picked up her Kinetic and made for the college. Even though she was suspended, she had to come to college to while her time away. Her mother must not know.

As she drove, still trying to calm her paced up heartbeats, she tried to connect all the events that had recently happened.

'Everything was fine till I told everything to Dr Bhasin,' she thought. 'I must tell Rahul and Gurkirat.'

Rahul and Gurkirat woke up past the mess timings for breakfast. So, they decided to go out to eat something. When they were about to leave, the mess boy told them that someone on the telephone wanted to speak to Rahul. Upon getting the message, Gurkirat and Rahul went towards the hostel's reception. There was noise on the other end as Rahul struggled to listen to the caller.

'Hello! Who is it?' Rahul asked.

'Am I talking to Rahul?' the caller enquired.

'Yes!' Rahul replied.

'I'm sorry to break this to you Rahul, but your mother tripped and fell, hurting her head quite badly when she got off the train at Amritsar railway station. She has been taken to Jhakhar Hospital. We got this phone number from her purse. You must reach there immediately,' said the caller and hung up before Rahul could ask anything.

Evidently, he was left panicked. His hands trembled as he put the receiver back.

'What happened Rahul?' Gurkirat asked.

'My mother....' he said as tears started flowing from his eyes. Rahul, the only son of his parents had had an underprivileged childhood. He had lost his father when he was just ten years old and was raised by his mother, who had worked very hard to pay for Rahul's education. She meant the world to him.

'We have to go Jhakhar hospital,' Rahul said in a trembling voice and ran towards the main gate of the college without a second thought. Gurkirat, sensing that something was not right, borrowed a passer-by course-mate's motorcycle and followed Rahul. Rahul hopped on and the duo took off. On their way to the hospital, Rahul told him everything the caller had said.

'Your mother came here without informing you?' Gurkirat asked.

'She had been telling me lately that she wanted to visit Amritsar. Maybe she thought of giving me a surprise,' Rahul replied.

Daringly yet carefully manoeuvring through traffic, Gurkirat stopped the motorcycle in front of the emergency ward of Jhakhar Hospital. They headed towards the reception and Rahul enquired about the accident case. The duo was directed to the emergency OT. When they both reached outside the OT, panting heavily from the sprint, a doctor came out and took them inside. Inside, they were baffled to see that the bed was empty and two doctors who had covered their face with masks stood in a corner.

'Hello Rahul!' said one of the doctors.

'Where is my mother?' Rahul asked.

'She is safe,' the doctor said.

'But where is she? I want to see her,' Rahul demanded.

Both the doctors exchanged looks, though no one said anything. When Gurkirat questioned them too, the two doctors removed their masks. They were none other than Chandu and Raju.

'Welcome back, Mr Rahul. Your mother is safe at your home,' said Chandu. Before the students could react, three more men suddenly entered the room. Rahul's eyes widened as he recognized the faces. And he knew that they knew who Rahul actually was. He wasn't the poor donor he had once pretended to be when he had met them. Rahul and Gurkirat, who didn't expect the sudden assault, started getting blows from all directions as men began to beat them. Rahul fell to the ground, but Gurkirat managed to fight them back, only partially though.

No sooner did he find a chance to push all of them in one corner than Rahul quickly got up and the two managed to escape that room. The duo ran to the stairs and down towards the exit. It was only when they were outside that they noticed nobody had followed them. They hopped on to the bike and went back to the college, where Kirti was already waiting outside their hostel.

'Those bastards!' said Rahul in anger. 'Why did they call us there? They could have attacked us anywhere.'

'That was the safest place for them.' replied Gurkirat. 'They just wanted to terrorise us, maybe give some sort of cautionary message. It's exactly what they did to Kirti.'

'The message is loud and clear. Someone wants us to stay away from the kidney scam,' replied Kirti. 'The attacks and our suspension is the first warning.'

'All this happened after we met Dr Bhasin,' said Gurkirat, looking straight at Kirti.

'You think he could be involved?' a distressed Kirti asked Gurkirat. Silence fell as they comprehended the complex, ground reality.

***

The seminar hall of Jhakhar Hospital was filled with staff members involved in the ever-increasing kidney trade. The administration of the hospital had called an emergency meeting. The key members of the hospital involved in the racket impatiently waited for the owner of the hospital, who was late by half an hour. It was one of those extremely rare times when the owner had himself come for a meeting. Chandu, Raju and Tinku proudly occupied the front seats. There were whispers all around. All of them enquired about the purpose of the meeting from one another.

Silence took over when the door opened. Dr Pawan Bhasin, along with two doctors and Ricky Bhatia, entered the hall. All the staff members stood up. Dr Bhasin gestured them to settle and took his position on the dais. He adjusted his oval spectacles, cracked his neck with a twitch on his face, pulled the sleeves of his brown blazer and switched on the mic.

'It is really shameful on my part that I have such employees in my hospital who breach my trust so easily. All I had asked you all was to maintain secrecy of our kidney business,' said a furious Bhasin in a rather calm tone. 'Some of you have been negligent enough. Do you know the serious consequences we have to face due to your negligence?'

The audience went numb for a while.

'All of you are like those irresponsible citizens out there,' he said, a little louder this time, 'who have a spare kidney, but won't donate it. That is why I started this business.' He took a pause as if reminiscing and then continued, 'People must donate kidneys. But they'd rather sell them. How pathetic! I believe we are doing a good job in the end by imparting kidneys to those who need it. And punishing those who would only sell it for money. That is why we cannot let punishments befall on any of us.'

Most of the audience couldn't draw any meaning out of this logic. And yet they listened.

Chandu and Raju didn't care about what was being said. They were simply awestruck to see the actual mastermind of the entire illegal organ trade for the first time.

'You people form a system, a system which was strong when I put it in order. But it has grown so weak that only three young students and a retired lawyer could almost expose it!' Bhasin shouted this time, 'Had they not come to me, I wouldn't have known anything. This would have been over.' Bhasin's eyes were incandescent with anger, his beard full of droplets he had spat out while shouting.

He took a deep breath, ran his gaze through the audience which had almost frozen in fear and gulped water from the glass kept on the dais. Tinku, who could be easily spotted, owing to the bright white color of his suit, sank in his seat, avoiding eye contact with his master.

'Sir, we have already apprehended the lawyer and destroyed all evidences. We were after the students, but they met you before we could do anything,' Ricky Bhatia, who stood beside Bhasin, spoke softly yet confidently. 'Kindly forgive us this time! I assure you that this will not be repeated.'

'Keep an eye on the students and teach that lawyer a lesson of his life. And patch all the loopholes they exploited to get into our system,' said Dr Bhasin and stomped out of the room. The audience heaved a sigh of relief.

Chapter 6

November 2000

Kirti, Rahul and Gurkirat discussed the recent events for hours. Finally, they arrived at a conclusion that they should halt their activities for some time, just in order to stay under the radar for a while.

'I think I should go home once. I am longing to see my mother,' Rahul said plainly. 'Especially after that prank or whatever it was.' Before Rahul could say anything any further, he felt a comforting touch sliding up his wrist towards his fingers. It was Kirti. From the beginning of this entire episode, they had come a long way, enough to show each other how they actually cared about one another. They knew now that their chords were in sync. They'd seen each other in their worst and they were aware about the strength of each other's character. More than that, they had stuck together. Affection was mutual this time, one that was beyond what friends were supposed to have. However, acknowledgement of the same remained a pending affair.

'Even I am feeling homesick. Nothing much to do here anyway,' replied Gurkirat.

'What about Manjit bhaiya?' a concerned Kirti asked.

'We will find him for sure! But first let things settle down for the time being. You know we are being watched. Any movement will draw their attention. Manjit bhaiya is a strong man and I'm sure he can look out for himself,' said Gurkirat.

'He is right! We can continue our efforts again after a few days. Let the culprits think that we have given up,' Rahul said, his hand still unmoving under Kirti's.

'But I am worried about Manjit bhaiya,' Kirti said.

'Nothing will happen to him. He is a fighter. I am worried more about you. For the next few days, you will be alone while we are gone. So stay alert and safe. In case of any emergency, don't hesitate to call me on my home number,' said Gurkirat.

'Don't worry, I will take care!' replied Kirti.

That evening, the boys packed their bags and left for the railway station. While Gurkirat's journey was merely of two-and-a-half hours, Rahul spent more than twenty hours to reach his hometown Patna. Kirti, as guided by Gurkirat, decided to stay home until the duo came back.

***

Tinku had a busy day in office. Repeated overseas calls on his mobile phone had made him forget his lunch. The middlemen in Canada wanted to send some kidney patients to Amritsar for kidney transplants. It was a big opportunity for Tinku as his efforts for establishing an overseas network were about to turn fruitful. He received patients' reports through fax and took it to doctors for consultation. After getting the final go ahead from Ricky Bhatia and Dr Bhasin, Tinku called his agent to send the patients. The biggest challenge for them was to show all the NRIs as the residents of Amritsar, Jalandhar and Gurdaspur, as the authorisation committee was not allowed to clear the cases of people living outside these districts. Tinku called Chandu and Raju for a meeting.

'Quickly find out some advocate who can prepare fake IDs and affidavits for our NRI chickens. But remember, do it cautiously! Majority of them are very honest in their profession,' Tinku said as he rolled a parantha, carefully dipping it in a glass of milk before stuffing all of it in his mouth in one go. He chewed slowly, without worrying for the milk droplets dripping on the contours of his pearl white sweatshirt on the belly, savouring the taste as his eyes rolled up in satisfaction.

'We have one already. Why do we need another?' a curious Raju asked.

'The one we have is buried in paperwork regarding the local customers. The flight of NRIs would reach anytime and we need to prepare their papers quickly,' Tinku replied, as he rolled another parantha.

'I know one! He will be willing to work,' said Chandu, happy at the prospect of providing a solution to his boss in exchange for some brownie points. Tinku nodded and gestured a thumbs up towards Chandu.

'Anything else we can help you with?' asked Raju.

'Both of you will personally take care of all the NRIs after they arrive. Make sure everything goes well. This is our first international assignment and it should be completed smoothly. Here is the list of blood groups of all the patients. Arrange the donors quickly,' said Tinku, handing over a piece of paper to his subordinates.

'Yes bhaiya ji,' Chandu and Raju replied in unison.

***

The first chartered flight landed in Amritsar with tenty-two patients from Canada ten days after Tinku's rendezvous with his middlemen. The patients were operated at Jhakhar Hospital and all the people involved in the racket made huge profits due to international currency involved.

As planned, they were shown on paper as the residents of Amritsar and its neighbouring districts in front of the authorisation committee. In subsequent days, patients from UK and other countries also got their kidney transplants done in Amritsar. The racket spread beyond Indian borders now.

Tinku dealt with all the international middlemen and fixed the deals, while Chandu and Raju took care of all the formalities of the patients when they arrived in India. The paperwork forgery was immaculate. The accent of the NRIs could have created a problem, but the authorisation committee seemed to have ignored it anyway. The increasing need for donors led to more booby traps, forceful apprehensions and even mysterious disappearances and deaths.

One morning, while on his way to receive an NRI customer at the airport, Raju received a frantic call from the safe house that two donors had died.

'Sir, what do we do with the corpses?' a newly-appointed doctor asked. He had entered into the racket recently for the monetary benefits attached.

'Send them to the hospital mortuary,' Raju replied casually, sitting in the taxi, striking off a row of crossword puzzle in the newspaper.

Nathu, the tea-seller friend of Hardial had a donation box installed at his stall. He would often say that he had undertaken to collect funds to help poor people in need. His customers liked his humanitarian nature and used to put pennies in it. He now owned a mobile phone with the justification that people could reach him easily in case of requirement of any emergency funds. No wonder the tea seller gained immense respect. Hardial had always liked this about him.

'Hello,' Nathu answered the phone when it rang.

'Nathu! Meet me in the evening. It is quite urgent,' the caller said. It was Chandu's voice on the other end.

'As you wish bhaiya ji,' Nathu agreed to meet him.

In the evening around seven, Nathu quickly shut his counter and went to the Company Gardens. He approached the fountains throwing water to an amusing height, took position under the statue of Mahatma Gandhi behind the fountains and waited for Chandu, who arrived fifteen minutes later.

'How is the Robin Hood?' Chandu said, with sarcasm dripping from his tone.

'I am prospering in your reign,' replied Nathu with folded hands.

'More bodies are piling up. Make arrangements for their cremation,' Chandu said.

'You need not worry. I will do the needful,' replied Nathu.

'Here is half the payment in advance,' said Chandu and handed Nathu a packet containing money. Nathu took it and put it inside his kurta's pocket immediately. There was a broad smile of gratitude on his face.

'And by the way, you did a good job with that rickshaw-wala Hardial. Keep pointing out such people to me,' Chandu patted Nathu's shoulder as he walked past him.

Frequent visits, interactions and allurements of Chandu had made Nathu a part of the ongoing kidney scandal.

Chandu had found such tea stalls and small shops the perfect spots for luring poor donors. Nathu took the donors' dead bodies from the mortuary of Jhakhar Hospital and cremated them as unclaimed at Sakuntala Mandir cremation ground. To avoid himself of being suspected by anyone, he had kept the donation box at his stall. He never hid his work, but openly told everyone that he had cremated unclaimed bodies through the collected funds and garnered praise for his social service.

***

Manjit was locked up inside a dimly-lit room of a deserted rice sheller, bruised and beaten. It had been days since he saw sunlight and his body felt fatigued and weak. Except for a plate of food which slid in twice a day from under the door, Manjit had no other routine visits. It was as if someone was trying to break him. He wanted to escape, but was unable to find a way, despite all his efforts. He shouted and beat the only door of that room every day, but it never yielded any results. Nobody ever came to even listen. He had lost his sleep; he had lost the track of time. He would often try to think and establish a connection between the events that led him to where he was. This was for the second time in his life that he had invited trouble, just because he had decided to help someone. Previously, till five years ago, when Manjit practised law in Amritsar court, he used to help solve the cases for poor people pro bono. A poor farmer had once come to him, seeking help in a land grabbing case.

'You don't worry. I will help you,' Manjit had agreed to the farmer's request at once. 'Just tell me the details.'

'I own just two acres of land in Tarn Taran. Couple of days ago, early in the morning, when I went towards my field, I was baffled to see that someone had constructed a boundary wall around it overnight,' the farmer had said.

'You didn't do anything?'

'I tried to enter inside, but was thrown away by some men who looked like guards. When I shouted, I was trashed badly. With the help of the village panchayat, I filed a complaint in the local police station, but they didn't register the complaint because the person who had grabbed my land showed some papers which proved that he was the original owner of the land.'

'Don't you have papers in your name?' Manjit had enquired.

'He is a wealthy man, brother,' was all that the farmer had said before taking out a bunch of old papers from a polythene bag.

'What is his name?' Manjit had asked.

'Tinku Yadav,' the farmer had replied.

'Who told you about me?' Manjit had asked him.

'Good men are rare. It is easy to find a man people praise so whole-heartedly,' the old farmer had said with a glint in his eyes.

Manjit had given some money from his wallet to the poor farmer. He had also assured him of help. A case was filed by Manjit and the trial had been scheduled a few weeks later. Within two months, Manjit's strong arguments and evidences had weakened the defendant's claim. For the final hearing, Tinku had been summoned by the court. Before appearing in the court, Tinku had come down to Manjit's chamber.

'You will not get any benefits by winning this case. The good often die poor. It would be better to withdraw the case and I will give you a blank cheque. You are free to fill any amount you desire,' Tinku had offered Manjit.

Manjit had simply walked past, laughing at Tinku's desperate efforts.

This had enraged Tinku so much that he had Manjit threatened with dire consequences.

On the very next day, based on the arguments of both sides, the judge had given the decision in the poor farmer's favour. Manjit's efforts to help the poor farmer and the first ever legal defeat suffered by Tinku had been the last straw. Tinku had ordered an assault on Manjit to teach him a lesson.

It was staged to look like a car accident. Manjit had lost his wife. Tinku had considered it as collateral damage. Manjit had tried to fight Tinku legally, but he didn't have enough evidence against him. All his efforts to get Tinku convicted had failed badly. Manjit was a man daring enough to kill Tinku single-handedly, but his respect for the law had held him back. Moreover, his wife's death had weakened him. Consequently, he had decided to give up and had ultimately stopped practising law.

History was repeating itself this time as well. His intentions of helping the poor man had put him in grave danger. Held captive in a dungeon since weeks, clueless about the culprits, Manjit had an intuition that it was connected to someone very powerful.

***

Gurkirat had been enjoying his stay at his home in Ludhiana. His family – a farmer father, a homemaker mother and a younger sister – was elated to have him back. They were simple folks and Gurkirat was glad to spend time with them. He often went around the busy industrial town and met his friends and relatives. Poori chhole from his favourite shop in Ghanta Ghar was his regular breakfast these days, sometimes even lunch and dinner. The only thing he missed about Amritsar was its lack of noise and traffic, which was a rare commodity for the residents of the busy city of Ludhiana.

One of his best friends from school, Rabaab Shergill, was an MBBS student at a local college in Ludhiana. When he went to meet him, he couldn't resist himself from telling Rabaab about the ongoing kidney scam and all that had happened with him and his friends at Amritsar, excluding sensitive details. It came like a bolt from the blue for Gurkirat when Rabaab revealed similar happenings in Ludhiana as well.

'The kidney business is not only restricted to Amritsar, Guri. It has also spread its wings in Ludhiana. More than six hundred transplants have been done here so far,' Rabaab said remorsefully.

'What? How do you know about it?' a shocked Gurkirat asked.

'Since you are my best friend and since you too decided to tell me all about it, I will also tell you what I know. But please don't share anything about this with any of your friends in Amritsar,' Rabaab said. There was a visible shame reflecting from his visage when he said, 'I think I too am involved in it somehow.'

'Do you have the slightest idea about what you are saying?' Gurkirat retorted.

'Please don't judge me,' Rabaab said, his turbaned head drooped down. 'I can't keep it from you, now that I know you know more about it than anyone else. But you must understand that I am stuck in the system. Not only me, but many other students are also indirectly involved.'

'But, how?' Gurkirat asked.

'We are compelled to take care of the partially-recovered donors by the college authorities,' Rabaab said.

'Why don't you refuse to do so?' Gurkirat asked.

'Grades, my friend,' Rabaab said. 'They bribed the underperforming students like me with grades. After all, it's MBBS we're talking about. It's not easy for an average student like me. And once we took the bribe and started doing the work allotted by them, there was no going back. They threatened that if any of us backed out, or complained against them, we will be equal perpetrators and our careers will be finished too.'

'But you could have quietly reported it to the police.'

'Haven't you tried it already? What did it yield?' Rabaab asked. Gurkirat could empathize with Rabaab. After all, he was just stuck in the scheme of bigger things. The culprits were at large and their connections were strong. Gurkirat knew it too well.

'Don't worry, Rabaab. I will keep this conversation a secret,' Gurkirat assured. But for the first time, he deviated from his word when he called Rahul and Kirti and discussed Rabaab's revelations with them upon reaching home.

They both were equally shocked to hear about the grim story of Gurkirat's friend, but guided Gurkirat not to speak about it to anyone as that would be in best interest of his friend. They reminded Gurkirat how dangerous the people running the scam were. Silence, for now, was the only guard.

***

Manjit could faintly hear vehicles approaching and halting near his room. The sound of the running engines echoed inside the walls of the empty sheller. Within the next few minutes, the door opened and two men started to walk inside. A visibly weak and half-conscious Manjit was then dragged by two men in front of Ricky Bhatia and Tinku. He was made to sit on his knees and one of the men splashed water on his face. Manjit partially regained his consciousness.

'So, we meet again, Manjit Singh,' Tinku said, taking the hood of his white sweatshirt off. 'I hope you haven't forgotten me.'

Manjit did not utter a word and just managed to lift his head to gaze all around. His long hair went in all directions in the absence of a turban. His face, bruised and beaten, had weakened so much due to the lack of food and sleep that all one could see on his face was his beard. Ricky Bhatia stepped forward and cupped Manjit's face in his hand aggressively. He lifted his face and began to talk.

'You thought you will get away easily? Our men were behind you since the day that sardar student had entered the safe house,' said Ricky Bhatia. 'How do you think we have been surviving for so long?'

'Was the previous lesson not enough for you? You shouldn't have come in my way again. Last time, the damage was unintentional. But this time, I will not spare you easily,' Tinku spoke in a hateful voice. 'All the evidences you had collected are already destroyed. You are left with nothing. It won't be difficult for us to kill you now. Nobody would come to know.'

'Then go ahead, what's stopping you?' Manjit retorted in a low, struggling voice.

Annoyed with Manjit's arrogance, Tinku took a pistol out of his pocket and pointed it at Manjit's head. Ricky Bhatia immediately tugged at his hand. He knew that killing a social activist at this point of time might trigger a mammoth investigation.

'Manjit Singh! I'd rather offer you a deal,' Ricky said, as he gestured Tinku to keep the gun back in his pocket. 'Stop helping those medical students and we will give you enough money to go resettle anywhere out of Punjab and live anonymously.'

'I am... ready... to take the money,' Manjit replied, struggling to breathe.

'See, everyone has a price tag,' Tinku commented.

'Just give me the money you promised every donor, along with the list of those donors. Also, it should include the compensation for those who died. And now that you're bountiful enough, write a written confession too,' replied Manjit.

This further enraged Tinku, who started kicking Manjit, felling him on the ground.

'You know me already, you scumbag! If you think you can stop me while I'm alive, you are mistaken,' Manjit spoke in between the beating.

Tinku desperately pulled Manjit's hair and shouted in his ears. He would have killed Manjit by now if Ricky wouldn't have been there.

'There is no need to kill him. He likes helping the poor and miserable, so let's make him one,' Ricky said as Manjit fell unconscious again.

'And what about those smartass students?' Tinku asked.

'Their souls will dread the consequences when they see their mentor,' said Ricky as he gestured his men to take an unconscious Manjit again in the room and lock him up.

Manjit woke up again after a couple of hours. When he opened his eyes, he found himself in a hospital room. A sudden gush of sharp pain in his abdomen and a sewed incision wound made Manjit realize that his kidney had been removed. Helplessness took the better of him and his eyes welled up. He tried to get up, but the severe pain pulled him back onto to bed. There was no one else in the room. Too weak to make any movement, Manjit managed to scream. The hospital staff came running inside.

'Get me out of here!' Manjit shouted at the nurses.

'Sir, we can't allow you to go anywhere. You are under recovery,' replied one of the nurses.

'You bloody cowards!' Manjit scoffed at the young boy, who exchanged confused looks with the other nurse.

'We are just employed here for post-operative care,' said the nurse.

It was as if Manjit had subconsciously comprehended the possibility of such consequences. He knew his future was ill-fated. He did not say a word after this and succumbed to the tranquilizer's effect, falling asleep with a sense of acceptance of the inevitable.

Chapter 7

Sucha Singh sprinted with his stick glued to the ball as he maneuvered like a wizard in the field. Soon, he was blocked by four opponents. He gazed back. All his mates were out of clear reach. He struggled, but somehow managed to dodge the four boys. Running with full speed, he aimed and took the shot. The ball rammed into the net with full speed before the goalkeeper could even move. It was a smooth goal. Just then the bell rang, indicating the end of the match. Overjoyed, Sucha laid on the ground, breathing heavily, as the last-minute effort had made his team the winner of the Zila Hockey tournament.

A seasoned player, the tall, lean Sucha had been the captain of his school hockey team before he had dropped out of school. His tanned body was the testimony to all those years of his regular practice in the sun. Even though he wasn't playing in the school anymore, his love for the game always took him to the local sports ground in his village Muradpura in Ludhiana, where he was usually hired by teams to coach and even play from their side. Seventeen years old, Sucha was the younger of the two sons of his parents. The income from two acres of farming land was not enough for his father to support the education of both children, so he had decided to spend on the one who was good in studies. Sucha had willingly volunteered in the favour of the family's decision. Sucha often accompanied his father to the fields where he was treated like a labourer. At times, it went to his heart that his father considered the studious son better than the one inclined to sports, but Sucha never spoke anything about his feelings and always obeyed his father's orders.

Hockey rejuvenated him, and he would manage to sneak out to play the game against his father's wish. His father often discouraged him by giving examples of famous hockey players who had ultimately died in poverty. Had it been cricket, his father would have been happier, as it had a better potential in the country than hockey. There were hardly any sponsors for hockey and limited audience for the matches. Ironically, the game where India became Olympic Champion eight times was suffering ignorance, just like those who played it.

Despite the negativity from his father, Sucha's love for hockey was unaffected. Every time he came home late after the match, he would be scolded by his father. Sucha's mother rescued him. She understood the sacrifice his son had made, but couldn't do anything. Sucha used to sleep on the terrace at night and would often gaze at the stars quietly for hours. Something simmered in his mind.

'There you are! We were waiting for you,' Sucha's father exclaimed with visible joy on his face when Sucha came home after the match one day. He couldn't believe what he had just heard. He was expecting a scolding. On the contrary, his father seemed overjoyed for reasons yet unknown.

'Have some laddoos,' his father said while opening a box full of motichoor laddoos.

'What is the occasion?" Sucha asked as he wiped his hand with his sleeveless blue jersey drenched in sweat and picked up a laddoo.

'Sarvan has secured 93% marks in BA second year,' his father replied.

'That's really good news!' said Sucha.

'I am proud of my son,' an elated father said. 'He will make me proud one day.'

Sucha felt embarrassed at the statement. His mother could feel Sucha quite didn't like his father's biased remarks. Sucha didn't utter a word after this and went upstairs. His mother followed him. It was the day Sucha broke into tears. He kept his head in his mother's lap and wept. She gently caressed her son's forehead with hands hardened by the toil of everyday life, wiped his tears with her cotton dupatta.

'Why doesn't bapu love me?' an innocent Sucha said, knowing the answer well.

'He loves you, my son. He just doesn't know how to express it,' his mother replied.

'But he knows exactly how to express when it comes to Sarvan,' Sucha retorted as he stopped crying.

'To motivate you,' she replied.

'Motivate?' he said.

'To make you compete for the same affection, pushing you to do something with your life,' his mother tried pacifying him, knowing it well that all Sucha had to do was play hockey, something he had already willingly given up.

Sucha was mature enough not to argue at this point. For a while he remained with his mother until she went to fetch him dinner, which he insisted on eating only if his mother fed him. She would love to do so every day, she said. Affection, the unavoidable need of mortals, was what Sucha needed in that moment.

By the next day, his mind had settled back into the daily routine.

Days passed and Sucha kept switching between sweating in the fields with his father during the day and on the hockey ground with his friends in the evening. On one such day, a fellow teammate broke the news of an upcoming hockey tournament where the winning team would be rewarded fifty thousand rupees as prize money. The chief guest was Sucha's idol, Olympian Ramandeep Singh, captain of Indian Hockey team. Excitement took the better of Sucha and he started preparing for the tournament along with his teammates.

It was a big opportunity, monetarily as well as for fame, which Sucha didn't want to miss.

Of course, he had to keep this development from his father. As the tournament edged closer, Sucha realized that evening practices alone won't be enough. He had to train to play when the sun was right over the head and the ground was far less humid. He decided to ask his father's permission to be spared from the farming work for a few days.

'What's the matter?' his father asked while eating missi roti with saag.

'I… uh… my team has to play a tournament,' Sucha replied, hesitantly.

'Do you know what time of year it is? We have to start preparing for the harvesting of crops before Baisakhi,' the father said, almost angrily as if triggered by the mere thought of Sucha playing some hockey tournament at that time of the year.

'I know bapu, but this tournament is very important to me,' Sucha pleaded.

'Nothing is more important than having food on the table. I don't have enough funds to hire labour. Forget the tournament. It's a distraction. Just go and sleep. You are going to the fields with me this week!' his father replied, almost sealing Sucha's fate.

'Just let me play this one! I promise I will not insist for another,' Sucha literally begged as his father got up from the cot in the open verandah of their house.

An adamant father did not respond and walked away, leaving the utensils to be cleared by Sucha.

Sucha had already made up his mind, though; even before this conversation. Whatever the consequences may be, he would face them. On the day of the tournament, he got out of home early in the morning, before his parents woke up. He went to the ground and started practising. Before long, his father discovered that Sucha was not at home. Knowing where he would be, his father too made way towards the tournament venue. Upon finding his son practising in the ground, Sucha was berated in front of his friends by a displeased father. In his rage, Sucha's father snatched his hockey stick and started hitting it on the ground and on a nearby iron pole, till it cracked.

The sight was unbearable for Sucha, who felt embarrassed in front of his fellow teammates, who stood there as stunned spectators. Without saying anything to his father, Sucha dashed away with tears in his eyes. His dream of playing in front of his idol already lay on the ground in pieces. As he made way towards home, Sucha made up his mind to run away from home. After taking out his savings from the jar kept in his room, he threw whatever he could find in a duffle bag. With his eyes still red, he went towards the railway station and boarded the first train, which was incidentally headed towards Amritsar. He didn't plan on a destination. He just wanted to leave. And he left.

Lost in thoughts, cursing his life, Sucha finally reached Amritsar in the afternoon. He decided that he would spend time by performing free *sewa* (service) at the Golden Temple, the epitome of Sikh faith. At least that would give him some satisfaction and also help his tumultuous thoughts to settle down. He began to walk from the crowded and noisy bus stand towards the Hall Bazaar, past the Suraj-Chanda-Tara theatres, ignoring constant calls of desperate hawkers trying hard to garner customers, finally reaching his destination.

As he stood at the crowded entrance of the Golden Temple, gazing at the sparkling white marble clock tower dome while other hasty pilgrims went past him, brushing their shoulders with him, he felt a sense of relief. The faint melodious sound of hymns playing at the tune of harmonium and tabla soothed his soul. He deposited his shoes at the *jodaghar* (shoe storehouse), washed his hands and feet, and entered the temple premises through a wide staircase under the clock tower dome.

Bright golden radiance of the Darbar Sahib covered with gold that stood in the center of the dark blue *sarovar* (holy pond) was the sight that Sucha had longed to see. Around the sarovar, on the marble periphery, men, women and children walked barefoot, with heads covered with either a dupatta or a saffron or white cloth, listening to the reverberating melodious hymns that filled the air.

A starving Sucha blessed Sikhism's idea of visiting the community kitchen before entering Darbar Sahib and filled his stomach with langar before offering his services in the same kitchen. For the rest of the day, he walked about the temple premises, mopping off the water from the marble steps after someone had had a holy dip, filling bowls of fresh drinking water on the counters installed in all four corners of the temple, or sometimes just sitting idle against a pillar along the periphery.

As the day wore to its end, Sucha booked a room in Guru Ramdas Sarai adjacent to the Golden Temple. From the next day onwards, Sucha would get up early in the morning, take a bath and go to the community kitchen to wash the utensils along with other volunteers, switch turns to cut the vegetables and would halt the service only to eat his own meals. Where Sucha's parents searched for him frantically, Sucha had found peace in his life.

One day, while working in the utensils area, Sucha' gaze fell upon a fair-skinned, brown-bearded, turbaned man, washing utensils with others. From the way he was dressed, he looked well off financially. Sucha asked him his name.

'Gurinder!' he replied. 'And you, young man?'

'I am Sucha Singh.'

The conversation ensued and Gurinder, who was almost twice as old as Sucha, befriended him. Gurinder told Sucha he had shifted to Amritsar from Jalandhar, owing to his business there. When Sucha disclosed the story of his life to Gurinder, his empathy towards Sucha garnered immense respect.

Gurinder's warmth and motivation comforted Sucha, who secretly wished he had an elder brother like Gurinder. By the time winters wore to an end, serving together, sitting and chatting for an hour or two had become an everyday affair for both of them.

'Have you been around this beautiful city? Did you try *Manu de Kulche*?' Gurinder asked Sucha one day.

'Never got out of these premises,' Sucha replied.

'Oh, then let me tell you *veere*, you are missing out on the best kulchas in the town. It's a sin not to eat a butter-filled kulcha with a glass full of *lassi* from Manu while you're in Amritsar.' Besides that, there is a lot to see here in Amritsar,' said Gurinder excitedly. Sucha wanted to tell Gurinder he didn't have enough money left to roam around, but refrained from doing so. Gurinder was, however, smart enough to understand.

'I can take you around in my Indica,' Gurinder offered. 'I'm anyway bored of driving around alone.'

'I... uh...' Sucha hesitated.

'Wear a nice turban tomorrow,' Gurinder brushed his beard with his fingers. 'We'll spend the weekend going around.'

'But what about the service?' asked Sucha.

'I'm sure Waheguru won't mind if you took a day off,' Gurinder patted on Sucha's shoulder in excitement.

The next day, as planned, Gurinder came and picked up Sucha from outside the parking of Guru Ramdas Sarai.

He took him to Lawrence Road first, where they had poori chhole at Novelty Sweets. After Sucha walked the entire length of Lawrence Road with Gurinder, with the dual aim to digest the heavy breakfast and watch all sorts of shops and showrooms on both sides of the road, they headed towards Khalsa College – an iconic building, a trademark of Sikh architecture which once used to be Maharaja Ranjit Singh's palace. Sucha was amazed to see the beautiful building. He envied the students who were fortunate enough to study there. The sight of a group of hockey players warming up in the front lawn brought back haunting memories and Sucha's smile vanished. A thoughtful Gurinder took Sucha away from there as they headed for Hall Bazar.

'Did you enjoy the day?' asked Gurinder when they dined at Bharawanda Dhaba, city's most loved restaurant with its heritage dating back to 1912. Two traditional thalis with tens of bowls filled to the brim with lentils and other vegetables cooked in desi ghee, and a pile of assorted breads hid the table underneath them.

'I enjoyed it to the fullest,' replied Sucha, 'and I must say you are a very good driver.'

'Thank you so much,' Gurinder went pink in the face.

They continued chatting over dinner. At the end of the meal, Sucha felt a bit uneasy as all the expenses were being paid by Gurinder that day.

'For how long will you stay at Golden Temple?' a curious Gurinder asked.

'Forever!' replied Sucha quickly.

'Be practical, Sucha! You have a long life ahead. You cannot just stay here like this.' There was seriousness in Gurinder's tone.

'This life is dedicated to Guru's service now,' replied Sucha.

'But the same Guru has said that we should work first and then chant his name. *Kirat karo, Naam japo...*' said Gurinder.

'*Vand chhako* (share, serve and eat),' Sucha completed the lines. He almost ignored what Gurinder had just said. Sucha took leave from him and went straight to his room in the Sarai. He could hardly catch any sleep. Gurinder's words echoed in his mind. Somewhere inside his head, he agreed to what Gurinder had said.

'Will you help me find a job?' Sucha asked Gurinder when they met in the community kitchen the next day.

'So, you did manage to come to your senses,' Gurinder said as he peeled potatoes. 'Don't worry, there's a vacancy for a driver. It should suit you. And the benefits are handsome!'

Sucha smiled and agreed and Gurinder scheduled driving lessons for him from the next day. Sucha was a quick learner and within three weeks, he learned enough to pass the test for his driving licence. Gurinder pulled some contacts and Sucha received his learner's licence in the fourth week.

Gurinder would now let Sucha drive his Indica too. One day, out of the blue, Gurinder said, 'Take me to Chandigarh.'

'What?' Sucha almost thought Gurinder was joking.

'You heard me right... and I mean it. Let's hone your skills today.'

Sucha's hesitation succumbed to Gurinder's insisting. Wherever Sucha felt nervous, Gurinder assisted him. However, after a few kilometers on the highway, Sucha realized driving on a highway was cakewalk. They reached Chandigarh after about five hours.

'Where to go now?' asked Sucha. Gurinder had taken the wheel before entering the city premises as traffic police was strict here.

'To one of my friend's house,' replied Gurinder. 'We shall stay for the night and head back tomorrow.'

Sucha could not believe everything that was happening to him. Never in his life had he thought he would get such opportunities and a real job. He thought of it as the instant by-product of his service at Golden Temple.

Gurinder took Sucha to his friend Suraj's apartment, who was an inspector in Chandigarh Police. He was warm and welcoming. Sucha noticed something unusual about Suraj. He didn't look healthy. His eyes were yellowish, his body lean and skin almost as dark and pale as if he had no blood left in his veins. Sucha couldn't contain his curiosity and questioned Suraj about his health as the three sipped tea in the common room of Suraj's apartment. Gurinder answered that Suraj was suffering from a kidney ailment.

'See how an ailment has changed the outlook of a six-feet tall gentleman,' Sucha exclaimed with empathy as he ran his gaze through the framed photographs of Suraj from erstwhile days. 'What do the doctors say?'

'They say that a kidney transplant is the only option left to save his life,' replied Gurinder.

In the meantime, Suraj arranged dinner at the dining table. After another couple of minutes, Gurinder initiated a conversation.

'Sucha, I have a plan for you, with which you will make more money than any other job. And you won't even have to work.' Suraj heated the vegetables in a frying pan, pretending not to overhear their conversation.

There was a look of curiousness on Sucha's face. Fate was being too kind to Sucha, and it wasn't usual.

'Donate your kidney,' said Gurinder straightway.

'What?' Sucha said surprised.

'Just give a kidney to Suraj bhaiya and you will get two lakh rupees...instantly,' said Gurinder. Sucha was confused. He didn't have a reply.

'Look, veere, Suraj is in need of a kidney. He doesn't even have any family. And you will be doing service to him, just like you serve the pilgrims at the gurudwara. But here, you get paid. Financial independence.'

'I can't do that,' replied Sucha plainly. 'I can't donate an organ.'

'It will not affect your health. You will continue leading a normal life,' Gurinder tried to convince him with an intimidating urgency in his voice.

Sucha might not have known much about medical science, but he knew well that after donating one kidney, he would never be able to play hockey. So, he was adamant. Repeated convincing by Gurinder reaped no results and this discussion made Sucha angry. He requested to take leave immediately.

'Give your kidney like a good boy and take the money, or it will be removed forcefully and you will get nothing,' a frustrated and impatient Suraj said from the edge of the dining table. He brandished a pistol. Sucha looked towards Gurinder, who sat on the sofa, silently. Gurinder, whom Sucha had trusted as a friend, was the commissioning agent of some middlemen of the kidney trade. Little did Sucha know that he wasn't the only one, but it was a common practice for Gurinder to befriend people like him in Golden Temple and lure them to sell their kidneys. Suraj was the police officer who used to help the middlemen. When he himself fell ill, he was promised a free kidney transplant by Ricky Bhatia. Sucha was taken to Chandigarh because his blood group, which Gurinder had asked him while taking his details for the job, had matched with Suraj.

Nobody batted an eyelid for a couple of moments and then Sucha dashed towards the exit gate. Gurinder caught him, and with Suraj's help, overpowered him. Sucha was yelling, but was locked in a room. Sucha's destiny was doomed, after all.

Sucha was kept as a hostage for a couple of days and then taken to a hospital in Jalandhar at gunpoint. After the completion of all the documentation and against his wish, his kidney was finally removed. He was discharged from hospital a few days later, still under recovery. Having no other place to go, a heartbroken Sucha decided to go back home. He could barely walk, but somehow managed to reach Ludhiana railway station. When he came out of the station building, a sudden wave of dizziness overtook him. He was about to fall when someone caught hold of him. It was Gurkirat, who was going back to Amritsar after visiting his parents. He made Sucha sit and offered him some water. Before he could ask Sucha anything more, the train whistled and he ran towards it. But the budding doctor understood from the symptoms and incision wound that Sucha had also been the victim of the kidney racket.

***

This time when Manjit Singh opened his eyes, he found himself in a moving ambulance. He tried to move, but was tied to the stretcher with belts. He saw two men sitting on one side. He questioned them where he was being taken, but none of them responded. Manjit was kept at the hospital initially and then at a safe house for a few weeks, like any other donor. All this while, he was given sedatives so that he could not create chaos.

The ambulance suddenly stopped and two men untied Manjit. One of them then opened the door and the other one pushed Manjit out. The ambulance then sped away. Manjit found himself on the outskirts of some city. Unable to figure out anything, he tried to stop some vehicles for help, but no one hit the brakes. He then walked for a couple of hours and entered the city. Upon asking someone there, he came to know that he was in Beas. He had no idea about where his kidney was removed. After a few more unsuccessful attempts, he managed to take lift from a truck driver and finally reached Amritsar.

On the way to his home, Manjit requested a shopkeeper for one phone call and contacted Kirti. He asked her to immediately meet him, along with Gurkirat and Rahul. When he entered his house, with one hand on his waist and another holding a stick to aid in walking, he was depressed to see its condition. Unable to muster strength to put the house in order, Manjit just dropped on his chair and closed his eyes. After about ten minutes, continuous thumping on the main door pulled him out of his nap. He struggled to stand and went outside in anticipation that it must be the students. But he was baffled to see half a dozen policemen.

'What is the matter, officer?' he asked.

'Just open the door! We have a search warrant for your house,' said a sub-inspector.

'We have information that you have sold your kidney illegally for money,' said the other policeman as they pushed Manjit aside to enter his house.

'My kidney was removed without my consent. Forcefully. I have not taken any money,' Manjit said, but no one listened.

Within the next few minutes, one of the men shouted that he has found a packet containing money. The accompanying officers rushed towards him and when the currency was counted, it summed up to five lakh rupees. The sub-inspector lifted the packet, staring Manjit in his eyes, 'What is this, Mr Advocate? Where did this money come from?'

'This is a conspiracy. I am being framed,' Manjit said, punctuating every word with his index finger.

The recovery of money and the removal of Manjit's kidney had given the police strong evidence to frame a case of illegal organ trade against him. When a handcuffed Manjit was being pushed inside the Police jeep, the students reached. As they neared the vehicle, with an expression of shock visible on their faces, Manjit gestured at them to stay away. In front of the helpless students, Manjit was taken away by the police, as his curious neighbours peered from their balconies and windows.

Chapter 8

Ricky Bhatia's mobile phone rang; he had been waiting for it. Tinku, who had been pacing up and down the private club room, stopped at once. When Ricky answered the call, the subscriber at other end informed him that his work had been completed successfully.

'That's great news sir,' said Ricky excitedly.

Both Ricky and Tinku raised a toast of happiness, the former with a bourbon and latter with piping hot milk.

'The only pain left in our behinds is those students, in case they decide to create trouble again,' said Tinku.

'Just do one thing that will act as final nail in the coffin,' Ricky advised. 'Call the parents of all three students and inform them what they have been doing. Also threaten them, but not directly.'

'Good idea!' Tinku nodded. 'These parents have given their children too much freedom. It's time they tighten them up a little.'

'And what about the people you picked up from my hometown, Tarn Taran?' Ricky asked.

'They all are recovering. Surgeries have been carried out,' replied Tinku.

'Good! Just take a bit of extra care of them,' Ricky said with a cunning smile.

'I will look, don't worry. And personally.' He took a sip from his cup and said, 'I wanted to inform you about one more thing. That newly appointed SHO in Tarn Taran is quite honest and is known for his clean record. I'm afraid if any of the donors approach him, things could go against us,' said Tinku.

'Don't worry! Nothing will happen. Power lies in money, not honesty. And moreover, he's just an SHO. We have our tentacles spread till his headquarter's headquarter. If he poses a problem, we'll get him transferred,' Ricky said, quite proud of his contacts.

***

Manjit Singh was produced in district court, from where he was sent on a fourteen-day police remand. There was no attention given to his pleas, because the entire system was corrupt. The person who had spent his life preventing innocents from going to jail was put behind bars. Kirti, Rahul and Gurkirat reached Sadar Police Station and pleaded the SHO to allow them to meet him, but they were not allowed. Kirti, stubborn as she was, was adamant. In the end, she could buy five minutes for herself.

Even though she wasn't the emotional one, she couldn't hold her tears back when she saw Manjit's condition inside the cell. His turban and shirt had stains of blood. His jaw and left eye were swollen and purple, as if he had been beaten. He was much weaker than Kirti first saw him. But the look on Manjit's face hadn't changed at all. His eyes still possessed the same resolute look. His face was still expressionless.

As Kirti blinked away her emotions, Manjit recited

everything that had happened with him in the last few weeks. Both were smart enough to understand that it was the job of the kidney scam kingpins. Kirti came out in five minutes and the trio left the police station premises.

They had made up their mind. They would do everything in their capacity to get Manjit out of jail. They needed to hire an advocate for that.

The next day onwards, the three began individual searches for an advocate. To their disappointment, due to lack of proof of Manjit's innocence, none of them agreed to take up the case. One advocate advised Rahul that he could apply for Manjit's bail on medical grounds, but he would have to hire some other lawyer to fight the case. The trio contributed the money for the lawyer's fees to file a bail application for Manjit. Even though the advocate mentioned strong arguments, but the plea was finally rejected by court on the day of hearing. They were out of options and ideas to get Manjit out of jail.

The next day, Kirti was surprised to see her father at the gate early in the morning. She wasn't expecting him until weekend, and definitely not in the middle of the week.

'Is everything alright? You didn't inform that you were coming,' her mother finally asked as she served breakfast. Kirti seconded the question.

'We have something serious to discuss as a family,' Kirti's father replied as he unseeingly stirred the cereal in his bowl. Both the mother and daughter threw a concerned, questioning gaze at him.

'Someone called on my office number and told me what Kirti has been doing since a couple of weeks,' Mr Sharma said.

'And we as parents remained in oblivion.' A chill went down Kirti's spine as she wondered if it was about the kidney scam.

'What has she done?' asked a concerned mother. 'Did she break someone's nose again? Did she fail in some exam? Is she dating someone?'

Kirti tried to look away.

'It would have been okay if it were any of these options,' her father said as he looked at Kirti with a visible disappointment in his eyes. 'But the caller wasn't just another normal person. He warned and even threatened me with Kirti's life.'

Kirti understood that it was exactly what she had feared. Knowing that she couldn't hide anything from her parents anymore, she took charge of the conversation and told her parents everything.

'How could you even think that you and your friends, along with some psycho advocate, can fight some gangsters?' Kirti's father asked, almost losing his calm.

'We just intended to help one poor person, papa! We didn't know that the racket will be so big,' Kirti replied.

'We send you to college to study medicine, not to learn how to become a detective,' said Kirti's father in anger. 'Indulging in all these activities will not only spoil your future, but also put you in grave danger.'

Kirti did not utter a word.

'Look, you are our only child and we can't lose you beta,' her father said softly, voicing his concern.

'You have to promise us that you will not indulge in any of these activities anymore,' said Kirti's mother.

Kirti remained quiet. No one spoke anything for a couple of minutes. Tension filled the air.

'You are an intelligent girl. We have only you as our child. Where will we go if something happens to you?' her father said, almost pleading.

'Nothing will happen to me papa,' replied Kirti, realizing her unfairness towards her parents' dreams.

'So, you're saying you won't repeat anything like this?' asked her mother.

'No... but I... if only,' Kirti stuttered.

'No ifs and buts! You have to stop this, understand?' Kirti's mother lost her cool.

Silence took over once again. Conflicting thoughts plagued Kirti's mind in that moment of silence. She never wanted to give up at this point, but at the same time, she felt worried about the fact that her father was threatened by those goons. To relieve her parents, she knew she had to give them her word.

'Ok, I assure you I will not indulge in this anymore,' Kirti said.

'That's my good girl,' Kirti's father heaved a sigh of relief.

On the same day, Gurkirat's father and Rahul's mother also received similar phone calls. They were both scolded over the phone by their parents. Gurkirat's father got so annoyed and upset that he told him to pack his bag, leave the degree and come back to his home in Ludhiana. It was only after repeated requests and assurance by Gurkirat that he would not indulge in such things anymore that he was finally allowed to stay back at Amritsar.

Rahul couldn't hear her mother weeping over the phone, so he immediately gave her his word. Once again, the trio felt helpless. It felt like the end of the road. These people knew well about their families. After seeing what Manjit had gone through, they knew that any harm could befall them.

They didn't understand how to proceed further. Failure to find an advocate and pressure by parents anchored them down. All doors had shut. They knew that one wrong move in the coming days could land them in trouble. So they limited their daily routine to attending lectures in college. They knew they were being watched. It was quite intimidating and scary. But somewhere in the back of their minds, each of them was still thinking of finding a solution.

'Media could be the solution,' Kirti mumbled these words out of the blue while the trio was having lunch in the college one day.

'Press?' A baffled Rahul said. 'I think you still haven't learnt any lesson from the attacks and the phone calls.' Kirti shook her head in disapproval.

'Listen to what she has to say,' Gurkirat interrupted as Rahul shrugged his shoulders.

'There is no other option left. Journalism is something we haven't yet explored,' replied Kirti, her eyes prying through the mess crowd to see if someone overheard them.

'They will come to know it's us if we tell the press,' Rahul commented, his eyes fixed at Kirti, admiring her kajal, as she still looked around. No sooner did her gaze fall back at Rahul than he looked away. But it was late, she had noticed.

'It's not necessary for us to be on the forefront. We can simply provide information and we have to find someone trustworthy for that. Let people know Manjit Singh's true story. If it kicks off, it might help in garnering public support for him and building pressure on the police,' replied Kirti.

'This seems to be a workable solution,' Gurkirat added. 'But… there's no going back from here. Are both of you sure about it?'

'Isn't this what we all want to do?' Kirti said as she looked at Rahul, who looked unsure. 'After all, we started this. We must finish this.' What else could Rahul have done than give in.

'I'm not scared,' Kirti held Rahul's hand right after Gurkirat went to dispose off his plate, 'and I don't want you to be scared. We're in this together.' Rahul's heart skipped a beat.

Gurkirat had a distant relative who was a local news reporter in Ludhiana, but he didn't want to contact him. He was afraid that he might inform Gurkirat's father. At the same time, he didn't want to let go of the only opportunity to save Manjit, who they thought was in this situation because of them. So, he finally decided to take the risk and contact his cousin. The cousin gave him the contact details of Baljit Rana, a news reporter from Amritsar, who was his friend and batch-mate.

Contrary to Gurkirat's apprehensions, his cousin praised Gurkirat for his selfless efforts and assured him of confidentiality. The same evening after college, Gurkirat and Rahul, without wasting any time, reached at Baljit's address near Khazana Gate, making their way through narrow crowded streets of the old walled city filled with pedestrians, motorcyclists and rickshaw pullers. The main gate of the house was answered when the bell was rung for the second time and a clean shaven specsy sporting a crew cut, who looked in his thirties, came out. After the duo gave him the reference, he took them inside.

It was an old pre-Partition house which had an open cubicle space in the centre, surrounded by marbled alley on the three sides with a roof supported by pillars. Towards the right of the open space, a bricked staircase took them to the first floor, where they were taken inside a room which was more like an unorganized office, with a desk in the centre and almost everything lying everywhere.

'Tea or lassi?' asked the man with spectacles as he tossed some diaries lying on the chairs to make space for Gurkirat and Rahul to sit.

'We're good, thank you,' Gurkirat said right in time before Rahul could place a demand.

'Then tell me how can Baljit be of help to you?'

After the basic introduction, Gurkirat and Rahul told Baljit everything that had happened in the recent past with Manjit. Baljit patiently listened to them. An hour flew by before the duo finished.

'And now we want you to publish Manjit Singh's story in your newspaper,' Gurkirat said in the end.

'Do you have proofs of your investigation?' Baljit asked as he cracked his neck sideways.

'We don't have anything right now except the details of the preliminary findings. All evidences were taken away and destroyed by the goons when Manjit bhaiya got kidnapped,' replied Gurkirat.

'My editor-in-chief will not allow me to publish anything without the evidences.' Baljit sighed.

'But you must do something,' Rahul pleaded, 'it's our only hope.'

Baljit kept thinking for a while. It appeared as if he wanted to help them, but the lack of evidence was a road block.

'Let me see if I can do something with the information of your preliminary investigation. Give me two to three days,' Baljit said.

Manjit's story had managed to move Baljit, who was a man true to his profession. The next day, Baljit decided to collect evidences himself on the basis of the findings of these medical students. After all, reporting crime was something he had been pursuing since he was nineteen. He went at the address of the safe house, but it was locked. The colony's watchman informed him that the house had been sold. He then visited Jhakhar Hospital, but couldn't find anything worthwhile to be used in his article. Nobody lent him an ear when he contacted the office of the authorization committee. He worked on it for two days, but found nothing. When everything else failed, he decided to contact Hardial, whose complaint had set everything in motion.

When he reached his house, he was disappointed to learn that Hardial and his family had already left the city, or might have been driven away. Despite his efforts, Baljit was unable to collect evidences to publish a story in the newspaper.

'There must be something that you can still do?' a hopeful Gurkirat asked.

'Since all other efforts have gone in vain, we are only left with one last option,' he replied.

'What option?'

'I must interview Manjit Singh in jail and publish it in the newspaper,' replied Baljit.

'Don't you think it can land you in trouble?' a concerned Gurkirat asked.

'I have been covering crime reporting since I was nineteen,' Baljit said in a flaunting tone. 'Threats, intimidation, I know it all. But we journalists know how to play our cards. You don't worry.'

The duo left his house with a hope that something positive would happen in Manjit Singh's case. Where the students prayed at the Gurudwara, Baljit managed to meet Manjit Singh in jail. He had his sources, so it wasn't difficult. He rushed to the police station and had just met Manjit when a police van arrived with a couple of police officers. In a haphazard attempt, as if on cue, they took Manjit out and pushed him in their van, citing that he was being shifted right before Baljit could begin with the interview.

It was a clear sign someone hand in gloves with the perpetrators had tipped them off. The one last effort to save Manjit Singh had now failed. Baljit was left disappointed and for the first time, even without talking to Manjit, he could feel his pain. He could feel the magnanimity of this scam. The students had tried everything they could for Manjit's release, but nothing worked.

The trio was left with nothing more than following their lecture routine in the college. Any deliberate efforts would reap harmful consequences and they knew it. Baljit Rana too got busy in his work and never tried to contact Manjit again or find his whereabouts until one day, as Baljit was working in his home-office, his phone rang. The caller, his faithful source in the police department, informed him that an FIR had been registered against Ricky Bhatia under Transplants of Human Organs Act in Tarn Taran.

Baljit, in pursuit of collecting evidence to get justice for Manjit Singh, had already activated his sources everywhere. He immediately got up and rushed towards Tarn Taran to get further details. It was the same SHO whom Tinku feared for his honesty who had filed the report. Baljit collected all the details of the FIR from him. The FIR was registered on behalf of an affidavit submitted by one of the kidney donors. He had alleged that his kidney was removed forcefully. The FIR also included the name of Tinku and another associate.

The SHO had already conducted raids to nab the culprits, but they had been absconding. Baljit had now got one evidence against Ricky Bhatia, and he wanted to use it to the fullest. He drafted a complete report on the basis of the FIR and at the bottom of it, he included Manjit Singh's story. After getting the final approval from his editor-in-chief, Baljit saw to it that his story was published on the front page in the next day's newspaper.

Within no time, the news became a breaking one. Everyone in the city woke up to the news about a kidney scam. The first reaction of the common people was that they started questioning the government.

Gurkirat, Kirti and Rahul felt surprised and happy when they read the news. Their efforts had finally paid off.

Where Manjit Singh's story garnered general sympathy, Dr Bhasin and his team got worried to death. The news wreaked havoc amongst the entire community of perpetrators. They knew that this could kindle a fire that they wouldn't be able to extinguish. They had to react! Dr Bhasin immediately called for an emergency meeting of his top associates.

'I am suspending all our activities for a few days. Everything else in the hospital will function normally,' Bhasin told his associated in the conference hall of the hospital. 'And it's better if everyone stays away from news reporters till everything is back to normal again.'

No sooner did the meeting was dismissed than Bhasin's phone rang. The display flashed a number with Nepal's ISD code.

'Sir, I am really sorry. I took that SHO lightly. I want to...'

'Sorry is futile now. Now do me a favour, and don't come back here till I call you. Also, keep that clown Tinku with you. Goodbye for now!' A seemingly annoyed Dr Bhasin said and disconnected the call.

***

News reporters thronged the police station to get comments of the station in-charge who had caught Manjit Singh, but he avoided any interaction with them. The leaders of the opposition party started making statements, asking the ruling government to nab the accused.

Baljit's article had worked. Things were beginning to turn in favour of Manjit Singh. The SHO of Tarn Taran, a simple, god-fearing turbaned officer almost on the verge of retiring, Kulwant Janjua, who had lodged the FIR against Ricky Bhatia was also interviewed by the media. All these events started building pressure on Dr Bhasin and his team.

Gurkirat and Rahul went to Baljit's home to thank him for his contribution. They praised him for his brave efforts. Baljit assured them that he would continue his efforts to bring justice for Manjit and others who had suffered. He planned to publish one more story related to the efforts of Kulwant Janjua to amplify the movement against the culprits. He took an appointment and went to Tarn Taran to interview him.

He reached the police station on time, but was told to wait outside for ten minutes. When he was called inside, he saw that the SHO was busy talking to someone over phone. He gestured Baljit to sit down.

'Sat Sri Akal Mr Baljit Rana! How are you?' asked the SHO when he hung up the phone.

'Sat Sri Akal, I'm fine sir! All thanks to your daring. Nobody else could have filed such a detailed FIR,' replied Baljit.

Normally, Baljit would have received an embarrassed thanks from the SHO, but he saw an unidentifiable concern on his face.

'So, shall we start the interview?' asked Baljit.

The SHO remained silent for two minutes, staring unseeingly at the tricolor insignia resting on his table and then leaned forward with a made-up smile.

'That won't be possible as of now, Mr Baljit. My transfer orders just came in. I have been barred from any media interaction,' said the SHO.

'What?' A baffled Baljit said.

'You heard that right,' replied the SHO. 'You guys may still have freedom of speech. Our freedom of action comes at a price. This time, I'm paying for it.'

Dr Bhasin had pulled his cards. Through his strong political connections, he had pressurised the senior police officials to take action against SHO Kulwant Janjua to suppress the case.

Baljit's interview of Janjua was extremely important to fuel the ongoing fire against the culprits. But he had no choice and left the police station, disappointed.

He shared the developments with Gurkirat and Rahul. The students feared something like this was bound to happen. It was a network of powerful people they were up against. Baljit didn't realize that he had put his head in the crocodile's mouth.

On the same day, as Baljit's editor-in-chief was about to leave the office, he received a phone call. It was from the office of the ruling party's MLA. The conversation lasted for about ten minutes and the editor-in-chief looked upset when he hung up the phone. Next day, he called Baljit Rana to his office.

'You have to stop covering that kidney transplant case of Tarn Taran and Manjit Singh's story,' the editor-in-chief instructed.

'But why sir?' questioned Baljit.

'Because I am ordering you to do so,' replied his boss, more strictly this time.

'But sir, I had published everything with your permission,' said Baljit. 'And look at the sales department data. We're getting new subscriptions at a rate we haven't seen before in the last few years.'

'I permitted because I didn't know that this would turn out to be so big!' replied the editor-in-chief.

'Is someone pressurising you?' asked Baljit straight-forwardly.

'I can't answer your questions. You have to follow my instructions... please,' the editor-in-chief had a look of helplessness in his eyes and Baljit recognized it well. The man wasn't one to be pressurised easily. But if someone had managed to do so, it had to be something out of his capacity, something undeniably big.

Dr Bhasin had struck back again, using all his arsenal this time. He had used his influence to pressurise the editor-in-chief for not publishing any news that would expose him. In the coming days, there was no further coverage of the FIR against Ricky Bhatia and Manjit Singh in any newspaper.

When everything appeared to be going in favour of Manjit Singh, Baljit was made helpless all of a sudden. His brave efforts did not fetch any justice as the final ray of hope was overshadowed by darkness.

Gurkirat, Rahul and Kirti were depressed as the news about the kidney scam died a slow death.

Chapter 9

Sucha Singh sneaked out of his house as everyone else slept. Barely walking with the aid of his inverted hockey stick, he went towards the outskirts of his village. When morning twilight started brightening the sky, Sucha increased his pace and reached the bridge over the canal. He looked back towards his village and all his life's memories flashed through his mind in a couple of seconds. He reminisced sprinting across the bridge early in the morning when he would practice for hockey matches. His heart sank at the fact that he wouldn't be able to do it anymore. He kept his stick aside and climbed on the railing of the bridge. Tears rolled down his eyes as he felt stinging pain in his abdomen. He folded his hands, closed his eyes, prayed and jumped into the stream.

Sucha was a non-swimmer. He didn't struggle in the fast-flowing water. It was when he started losing his consciousness that someone got hold of him and swam with him to the shore. It was the milkman who was on his way towards the city. Sucha regained consciousness after resuscitation by the milkman. A disappointed Sucha struggled to get up, hurling curses at the milkman for saving him against his wish. The milkman pinned him down and tried to calm him. After the milkman was able to pacify Sucha, he was taken home.

Though Sucha and the milkman who saved him kept this incident from his parents, they came to know about it from a couple of witnesses who had spread this news through the entire village. Upon confrontation by the parents, Sucha confessed to his act. This left the family shocked. Where a grieving mother almost fell unconscious, a helpless father locked himself in a separate room and cried.

His son's ailment had forced him to mortgage his land, and despite that, he was not able to bear the expenses of Sucha's post-operative treatment. He had also approached the police, but no one listened to him. Instead, they threatened him of Sucha's arrest for unlawful donation of his kidney.

Sucha's house was wrapped in a pall of gloom since he had come back after the horrible incident. Sucha's mother was recovering from the shock which Sucha's suicide attempt had given her. In the evening, while she lay in bed, she gestured Sucha to come near her. An embarrassed Sucha, trying hard to shroud his vulnerability, went and sat beside her as she held his hand tightly. A stream of tears flowed down her cheeks.

'Promise me, you will not do anything stupid like this in the future,' she muttered.

'It just felt like the right thing to do in that moment. I feel like I am a burden on this family. But I promise I will not hurt you,' replied Sucha and cried.

His father stood at the door of the room, witness to their conversation.

'You were never a burden, puttar,' he said to Sucha, who didn't have the courage to turn around and face him.

From that day onwards, Sucha decided to live and fight. Though his physical health was not promising, he started selling vegetables on a cart near the village bus stop to earn his daily bread and help his family. Within the next few days, Sucha recovered mentally as he started keeping himself busy. The little money he made helped him buy his medicines.

***

Manjit's story in the newspaper had earned him quite some fame inside the jail. Some of the inmates who empathized with him started taking care of him. Unavoidably, Manjit made friends inside the jail. Along with the inmates, head constable Sartaj Singh couldn't keep himself from admiring the wrongfully accused Manjit. His story had moved him.

In his early fifties, with just a year left for his retirement, Sartaj often brought food for Manjit from his home. Manjit too poured his heart out to him in the many conversations they would indulged in. Manjit was now on extended police remand for another twenty days, and he had started losing hope. Nothing had worked out in his favour. Consistent medication rendered him pale and weak. At times, he would lose all hope, but the warrior inside him kept him from giving up. Faith was what kept him going.

One morning, Manjit was taken to the interrogation room. The SHO who had filed challan for the FIR registered by Partap Singh was sitting there. Manjit was pushed inside and the door was closed. There was nobody else inside the room.

'How are you, Manjit Singh?' the SHO, Sanjay Beri, asked.

'*Chardi kalaa* (high spirits),' replied Manjit.

'Someone who successfully lured tens of people to sell their kidneys, making heavy profits has to be in high spirits,' Sanjay Beri said. Manjit threw a confused gaze at him.

'Trying to build a false case against me? Now I get it,' Manjit said, pulling himself a chair to sit.

'Then accept it… confess!' Sanjay Beri said.

'I will never accept a lie! You will never get a false confession from me,' Manjit was blunt.

'I have other ways to make you confess,' the SHO said and got up from his chair. 'But considering your condition, I am asking you politely'.

'Intimidating me won't help, Beri saab,' Manjit was adamant and fearless.

His words annoyed the SHO. He went around the table towards Manjit and slapped him. Manjit fell off the chair on the floor. The SHO began kicking him. He paused and asked Manjit about his decision, but he didn't budge. Knowing well that beating Manjit any further could kill him – which wouldn't be in his favour, considering the limelight Manjit's story has garnered – the SHO stomped out of the room in anger. His efforts to implicate Manjit in another false case went fruitless.

Acting upon the instructions received from Ricky Bhatia, he had come with a hope that he would get Manjit Singh's confession to frame a false case against him. It was one of the many attempts made by the police to get his confession. This time, though, it ended up brutally for Manjit. He bled from his nose and was rushed to the hospital. He felt severe pain in his back, fluids oozing from the incision wound. Manjit was treated and sent back to the prison after twelve hours.

Sartaj Singh was enraged at the inhuman behaviour of the SHO, but felt helpless. It was a roadblock for the student trio and news reporter Baljit Rana. How to proceed further was still unclear. In fact, the well of ideas had dried up for real this time. Nothing but a miracle was awaited.

A white Ambassador car mounted with a blue light on top stopped at SP City's office and the newly-appointed, six-feet-tall, clean-shaven Superintendent, with big handlebar moustaches and Ray-Ban screening his eyes, stepped out. He was welcomed with a bouquet of flowers by the junior officers and then taken to his office. The SP's neat, creased uniform clinging to his athletic body had a name-tab above the right pocket that read 'Partap Singh'. He was the same Partap Singh who was once a trainee in the police department in Amritsar and the first one to file an FIR in the kidney scam case.

No sooner did he take charge than he immediately called for a meeting of all circle officers and gave them a piece of his mind. He made it clear that all he wanted from them was honesty and any misconduct would be dealt with severely. Where his first interaction with his staff left some happy with him being appointed as the new SP, others were left concerned.

When Kirti, Rahul and Gurkirat read in the newspaper about Partap's appointment, they saw a ray of hope. They wanted to send Manjit Singh's story to him. Though news about the kidney scam had died away, the scandal was still fresh in Partap Singh's mind. He wanted to dig it further because he knew that the case was not handled properly after he had left. This was one of the reasons he had requested for getting posted in Amritsar. Little did the students know that they were about to work for a similar cause and Manjit would be the key to it.

Displeased at the forgery of the previously-submitted challan against the FIR lodged by him when he was a trainee, he called SHO Sanjay Beri in his office after lunch one day.

'Why did you remove names in the original charge-sheet?' Partap asked straightforwardly, without even asking him to sit.

'Which charge-sheet, sir?' Sanjay asked, innocently.

'You know the case very well. Don't try to be over smart,' said an annoyed Partap.

'Sir, I have filed so many charge-sheets this year,' Sanjay said with counterfeited innocence.

Partap understood his intentions of beating around the bush.

'The one related to the kidney scam,' Partap said. 'The one I had filed when I was a trainee.'

'A trainee under me, sir,' Sanjay said and stared at the ranks on Partap's shoulders. 'How time changes... sir.'

'Just give me the goddamn answer!' Partap banged his fist on the table. 'Because time has indeed changed.'

'I omitted those names because I didn't find any evidence against them, sir!'

Partap knew that Sanjay was lying. He also knew there was no point talking to him any further. After Sanjay left his office, he called three police officers.

As per the general feedback from the environment, Partap had found out that they were the most honest and dedicated officers in the police department. Partap had also kept an eye on them since his training days. Partap needed them in his team. The first one was ASI Iqbal Singh, a turbaned officer who was more physically fit in his late forties than some of the younger officers in the department. The second one was Inspector Gopal Krishan, a young man in his thirties, who despite his round, protruding belly – owing to his habit of eating samosas day in and out – was a champion golfer and a certified cyber security expert. The third one was another turbaned officer, ASI Sukhjeet Singh, taller and younger than the other two, fit as a fiddle, a former boxing champion notorious for his anger issues. Partap briefed them about the scandal and what had happened in the past. They were well aware about the scandal. Partap told them that he wanted to start the investigation afresh.

'I am forming a team of one of the best officers in Amritsar. I am giving you full authority for this investigation. But remember, you will directly report to me about this case. You have to keep all developments a secret. Understood?'

'Yes sir!' the three officers replied in unison.

'You have five days, and I want results,' said Partap. Thus, an investigation which would help turn the tables, as Partap envisaged, began.

The next day, the three officers came up with a plan and discussed the same with Partap in his office. Partap suggested minor changes and approved the plan. The three officers had already activated their contacts in the city to fetch information.

It began with the recce of the major hotspots of the scandal. The sources of the investigating team informed that major deals were struck in a garden near Jhakhar Hospital at Green Avenue, Company Gardens and the Blood Bank. The three officers decided to keep an eye at all these places. There was no sign of anything wrong for two days and the officers started to suspect the information provided by their sources. Nevertheless, they decided to keep an eye for another day.

Iqbal Singh was present at Green Avenue garden with an associate. Gopal Krishan, along with two officials, inspected the blood bank. And Sukhjeet Singh was present at the Company Gardens with his associate. On the third day as well, there was no sign of any activity until evening. They discussed the situation over a phone call. Iqbal Singh insisted that they should wait. To their luck, at around six in the evening, five men were spotted at Green Avenue garden and six at Company Gardens. Inspector Gopal Krishan too spotted three persons at the blood bank.

To investigate further, the cops briefed their associates and sent them near these people with the aim to strike conversation with them. A well-disguised team of associates did their job so well that within a matter of minutes, it was disclosed to them that these men were middlemen in the kidney trade.

The associates, who posed as poor people in need of money, somehow managed to sneak out of the conversations. Immediately, they informed the investigating officers about their discoveries. This became a major breakthrough for the team.

The next day, those middlemen were arrested in a lightning-fast raid and information was shared with Partap over phone. He lauded the team's efforts. An FIR was registered against the offenders and they were produced in the district court. The next day's newspapers were filled with breaking news of the police cracking the kidney scam case. News reporters published interviews of Partap Singh and appreciated his efforts.

Partap was happy with this big breakthrough in his first case as SP City, Amritsar. He received a phone call of IG Akash Gupta, who praised Partap for his efforts and out-of-the-box approach. While thanking the IG, Partap informed him that he would continue working hard to reach the actual mastermind suspects. The IG encouraged him, but strictly instructed him to keep all information confidential in all further developments.

News of Partap's feat reached up the chain and he received a DO letter[7] from ADGP[8] cum OSD[9] Saqib Ahmed.

Gurkirat, Rahul and Kirti almost danced at the sight of the newspaper's headlines. Manjit's freedom seemed like a possibility now.

***

Dr Bhasin received a call on his mobile phone and he let out a loud laugh. The caller on the other side was a source at the police station who demanded the remaining amount of money. By virtue of the information he had shared, Bhasin's work seemed to have been completed successfully.

When Dr Bhasin gave the news to his associates, they congratulated him on handling everything so quickly and intellectually.

The fourteen offenders caught by Partap's team were only poor donors. Everything was pre-planned and staged. When Partap's team was about to start the investigation, Dr Bhasin had been informed in advance. He knew that they would be

7 Demi Official letter, drawing personal attention in inter-government communication.
8 Additional Director General Police
9 Officer on Special Duty

keeping an eye at the probable sites and if they would not find anything, they would divert their attention towards other places and persons.

It was then that Bhasin instructed his associates to once again lure the poor donors by offering them the job of middlemen. The poor people had accepted the offer when a handsome advance amount was given to them. According to the plan, they were called for a meeting at Company Garden, Blood Bank and Green Avenue park at the time when the investigating team searched for the culprits.

Dr Bhasin felt that after their arrest, the case would die down once again. He would take a brief pause, and when everyone would eventually forget about the kidney scam, he would resume his business.

The culprits had managed to fool the police investigation team. Nobody listened to the fourteen donors for their side of the story and the donors knew there was no point shouting it out.

However, the suddenness of such a large-scale bust was something hard to digest for Partap, who continued to ponder over the events for the next few days.

'How could such a shady scam come to an end all of a sudden?' he said to himself as he sat in his office one day, rotating the paper-weight with one hand.

'May I come in, sir?' It was the peon at the door who disrupted Partap's thoughts.

Partap gestured him with a nod.

'Sir, there is a letter for you,' the peon said and handed over an envelope to Partap.

When Partap opened the envelope, there was a newspaper

cutting inside. It was the story which correspondent Baljit Rana had published in his newspaper. It also contained Manjit Singh's story at the bottom. When Partap read the clipping, he could comprehend that his apprehensions were right. Ricky Bhatia was still on the run. Tinku was not to be seen or heard. The recent arrests were stage-managed. The actual culprits were still at large.

'I need to dig deeper.'

The story of Manjit Singh caught Partap's attention. The man ought to know much more than what was given in the newspaper clippings, he thought. He immediately stomped out of his office in a hurry.

Partap met Manjit Singh in the jail. He pitied Manjit for his condition.

Manjit, who was almost fed up of meeting police officers every other day, refused to talk to him. When Partap showed Manjit the news clippings about his recent feat, stating that he knew it was all stage-managed by the culprits, Manjit decided to talk.

A sense of mutual confidence filled the air. After all, if an SP well aware about the scam and desperate to find answers had visited Manjit, there could be a possibility that Manjit's information could help him. An hour went by and Manjit Singh told him everything about the findings he and the students had managed to unearth. Partap was left baffled. He marveled at the enormity of sensitive information which Manjit and the students had gathered all by themselves.

'Maybe what I have found is just the tip of the iceberg then!' said Partap.

'I think you people have been deceived,' said Manjit Singh and coughed.

Manjit's grim condition was a live example in front of Partap about how horrible the aftermaths of such a criminal activity could be. He wondered how many poor people would have suffered, how many cheated and how many left to die. As a police officer, it was his moral responsibility to bring an end to it, he told himself.

The meeting with Manjit only acted as a catalyst for Partap and he vowed to get to the perpetrators, if Manjit was willing to help him. Determined and equipped with a 'do or die' attitude, Manjit agreed to help Partap. Partap called the investigating officer and asked about the charges levied against Manjit Singh.

'Sir, we recovered money from his house which he must have received for selling his kidney,' the officer said.

'Must have?' Partap retorted. 'Have you heard his side of the story? Has it been documented somewhere?'

'Sir... this man is a culprit,' replied the officer.

'Answer me!' said Partap, louder this time.

'No sir!' the officer replied faintly.

'How can you arrest and unnecessarily keep a physically ill person in prison for so long?' asked Partap, but the IO remained quiet.

'Make preparations to release this man,' Partap ordered the officer, who couldn't look him in the eyes anymore. Partap stared at Manjit for one last time and then left.

When SHO Sanjay Beri came to know about Partap's meeting with Manjit, he was irritated and enraged. But he could do little to avoid SP's orders from being implemented.

Manjit was released the next day. Partap made sure to send a vehicle to pick Manjit from the police station and bring him to his office. News about Manjit Singh's association with Partap reached the perpetrators and it posed a new challenge for them. Dr Bhasin, who had hoped that the case would shut for good, started exploring his sources to get rid of Partap. Manjit and Partap discussed about their next course of actions to unearth the scam.

'You need highly motivated and downright faithful officers for further investigation now,' Manjit suggested. 'These are powerful people we're up against, powerful enough to buy anything, even morals and principles.'

'I have the officers, you don't worry. What about those three students who had started the whole thing?' asked Partap.

'I will not involve them this time. All of them were attacked one by one. I can't put their lives at risk again,' replied Manjit. Partap nodded.

Manjit looked back at his life. He had been living all alone and was hardly left with anything to lose. It wouldn't make any difference if anything were to happen to him. But the young students had families and a whole life ahead of them.

Chapter 10

Rahul and Gurkirat rushed to Manjit Singh's house when Manjit called them and told them that he was out from the prison. Manjit was equally happy to see them, but didn't really know how to express it, so he thought of making them lassi.

Kirti joined half an hour later and was treated with a cup of tea. Even though the students had promised their parents not to see Manjit Singh anymore or go anywhere near this whole scam, but their admiration for Manjit Singh made them forget all the promises. The students couldn't help but notice how weak Manjit had grown while Manjit narrated to them how he got out of jail. The SP's support was a force multiplier and the students felt for the first time that their mission could now be headed in the right direction.

'It is time I fight the battle alone now,' said Manjit. 'I can't risk your lives again. This whole scam is dirtier than we imagined.'

'How can you say that our lives are at risk?' asked Gurkirat, unaware of the fact that Kirti had already told Manjit about the threat calls when she had met him in jail.

'I know about the incidents that had happened with you after I was kidnapped,' said Manjit and looked towards Kirti. Rahul and Gurkirat now knew about the source of his information. They threw disappointing gaze at an embarrassed Kirti.

'But we can't let you do everything yourself, given your health,' Gurkirat said.

'Nothing has happened to me. I am perfectly alright,' Manjit said and got up from the sofa to exhibit his recovering agility, but almost fell back before Rahul held him. His facial muscles twitched in the wake of severe pain.

'We can very well see how *perfectly alright* you are,' Gurkirat said, almost in a scolding tone. Manjit kept quiet.

'You will not fight alone. We stand beside you. The task which we had started as a team, we will finish it together as a team,' a determined Kirti said.

Manjit didn't utter a word. He fell short of words to convince the students to stay out of the events.

'We can take care of ourselves,' Gurkirat said, quite seriously, 'and we will take care of you as well, now that we know what we are up against. We couldn't do anything to save you then. The regret is ever lasting. But we won't back out now. It's the last mile.'

'So, you will not budge?' Manjit said.

'You taught us not to give up easily,' Kirti said.

'Alright then,' Manjit said and right when the students exchanged excited looks, he added, 'I will let you help me, but you have to promise me one thing.' The grins vanished for a moment.

'None of you will come forward. Partap and I will ourselves contact you as and when required,' Manjit said.

'Deal!' Rahul said at once. Gurkirat and Kirti followed, knowing there was no way around it.

After the immense pain and challenges they had stormed through, the team was back once again.

***

Partap Singh had lost his father at the age of eight and his mother had raised him and his two elder sisters all by herself. She would take up household chores in nearby localities in return for money, sometimes rations and clothing. Partap was a bright student and so, her mother made it an endeavour to support him in his education. Though his Mama, who lived in a village on the outskirts of Amritsar supported them by sending money whenever he could, it could never suffice.

When Partap completed his higher secondary education, he started tutoring students and forced his mother to retire. His sisters helped in running the house by stitching clothes. During his graduation, he would find time to take up odd jobs, sometimes a part-time accountant for a rice sheller, at times a delivery man for a courier hub, but he would toil day in and out to support his education and the family. He pursued his Post-Graduation in Hindi and cleared Civil Services Exam in the first attempt.

All his life, Partap had witnessed poverty and lack of privileges. It was only natural for him to empathise with the poor. Equipped with power and authority, when he passed out of the police academy, Partap had vowed to work for the betterment of the downtrodden. And as far as he had found out, the victims of this vicious kidney scam were all poor people, lured by middlemen with promise of money. How miserable they would be to sell an organ for a few thousand rupees, Partap would often wonder. And how evil of the men who would trick the poor into this scam. Where he could hardly do anything about their poverty, he knew it was well within his power to safeguard them against such life-shattering scams.

A meeting was set up by Partap and Manjit and the students were called as well. Partap instructed them not to be seen together and stagger their timings while setting off for the location he had given them. The place where Partap had called Manjit and the students was an old house in a village at the outskirts of Amritsar which belonged to his Mama. Partap's Mama, who didn't have children of his own, lived there with his wife. It was an old-fashioned yet elegant looking haveli with an open front verandah and cattle shed with two buffaloes tied in the barn to its right. A mechanical chaff cutter was kept in one corner and a vintage model Ford tractor was parked towards the left. When Manjit and the students reached, Partap was already present there. He had come alone in his private car. Partap humbly greeted the students and appreciated them for their efforts and the courage they had shown in unraveling the kidney scam.

After everyone exchanged greetings with the old couple, Partap took all of them in the room on the first floor while his Mami went to prepare tea for everyone. It was time for the students to share each and every detail of their investigation with Partap verbally. All this would have been simpler if they had the file prepared by Manjit Singh, but that had been destroyed by Ricky Bhatia's goons.

Kirti started her part of the story and told Partap how she had managed to sneak inside the Administrative Officer Ratan Lal's office, but found nothing.

'Why his office?' asked Partap.

'Because all files of kidney donations are kept in his office and I was looking for the file on Hardial,' replied Kirti.

Partap kept making notes in his diary.

'Sir, the reason why she did not find that file was that the donor's names are changed when they are presented before the authorisation committee. Fake affidavits are made and everyone from the lawyers to the magistrate are involved in the process,' said Gurkirat and told Partap the evidence he and Rahul had collected from the same office.

Partap had an inkling earlier that forgery of documents could be the reason that the authorisation committee approved the donations. The students had proved his hunch right. The conversation carried on with Partap asking meticulous questions about each and every detail the students had noticed. In the meantime, tea and homemade *mathhi* was lovingly served.

'So much has been happening in the city from such a long time and it is strange that it went unnoticed,' Partap commented.

'Because they have connections,' Manjit Singh said.

'It is only a matter of time until we get to these connections and break them,' Partap said.

It was Rahul's turn now. He narrated his experience at the Jhakhar Hospital.

'It started at the Blood Bank and ended at the Jhakhar Hospital. Chandu and Raju are the key middlemen of this trade. The hospital staff is equally involved. They were about to remove my kidney, but Gurkirat saved me,' Rahul heaved a sigh at the nightmarish memory of this incident.

The students told Partap about the attacks and the threat call.

'All this and the three of you are still here!' Partap said in an appreciating tone. 'Your efforts won't go in vain, I promise.'

'Sir, they treat the donors pathetically. I visited one of the safe houses and saw it with my own eyes,' Gurkirat said. Partap jotted down the address in his diary.

'The racket is not limited to Amritsar, sir! It had been running in Ludhiana as well,' Gurkirat added.

'This is a lot of information,' Partap scratched his moustache as he spoke. 'I will follow your leads. Is there anything more?'

'Sir! I have something to tell. We were suspended from college for one month and we still don't know the reason. But it happened after I met the famous kidney transplant surgeon, Dr Pawan Bhasin and tried to explain to him about the wrongful kidney trade,' Kirti said in one go.

'My knowledge about the man tells me that Dr Bhasin is quite a generous surgeon. He also treats the poor for free. Considering his involvement in the kidney scam just because he is a Kidney surgeon is only natural, but it cannot be ruled out completely. And the fact that firstly Rahul was taken to Jhakhar hospital and then both Gurkirat and Rahul were called there by the hoax caller only proves the involvement of Jhakhar Hospital in this scam. Since we do not have any documents or evidences to support the case, I will have to start from scratch.'

'I suggest that you and your team lie low for a couple of weeks. Let the culprits think that the police is satisfied with the arrest of fourteen offenders and the department is basking in its glory,' Manjit said.

'What purpose would that solve?' Partap asked.

'They will resume their activities without any fear, and when they think they have won, it will be the perfect time to strike,' replied Manjit.

'But don't you think they will get enough time to erase the records?' asked Partap.

'We cannot rule out that possibility, but the way they have acted in the past gives me a hundred percent surety that this idea will help us through,' replied Manjit.

'Let me ponder over it,' said Partap.

The meeting was over after almost two hours and before everyone got up to leave, Partap's Mami was ready with lunch. Though the students did not say it, but they were starving. Rahul was the first one to get seated for lunch on the cot laid in the verandah. Everyone else followed.

***

That night, Manjit received a phone call at eleven in the night.

It was Partap.

'I think you were right. Things should proceed the way you suggested,' he said and hung up.

Partap had been thinking about the whole case since the meeting. He was hell bent on getting to the bottom of the kidney scam.

Dr Bhasin – who was already worried about Manjit Singh's association with Partap – was told to suspend all illegal activities for some time by his 'higher' connection. Partap's honesty posed a risk for them. Where on one hand, the SP had decided to wait for a couple of weeks, on the other hand, the culprits had also made up a plan to suspend their activities for some time. Days passed and there was no action from both the sides.

As time progressed, the monetary losses suffered by Dr Bhasin piled up. He could not stop paying his team even when there was no trade being carried out. The only way he could progress was to know what was going on in Partap's mind. He sent one of his close associates in the police department to Partap's office to ask him indirectly if further investigation of the kidney scam was in progress. Partap denied the same and pretended as if he had almost forgotten about it. This was enough assurance for a desperate Dr Bhasin to resume his activities. In the test of patience, Manjit and Partap had won.

***

After Sucha's unsuccessful suicide attempt, his parents took special care of him. Though Sucha had promised never to repeat what he had tried, his brother, who stayed in the hostel, was called back home to stay with Sucha for some time. He would always try to keep Sucha happy and in high spirits. He would accompany him to the Gurudwara in the morning and to watch hockey matches in the local hockey ground in the evening. Sucha had slowly started recovering from his trauma.

Things had started to fall in place, but the cost of medicines was still a big burden on the family. So, his brother took up a part time job of a tutor in an academy. Gradually, the family scrambled out of the worst phase that they had lived through.

When Partap Singh and his team had nabbed the offenders involved in the kidney scam, the news had spread like wildfire in Punjab. Sucha's village was no exception. On one of the evenings, while Sucha and his brother were on their way back home from the hockey field, Sucha's erstwhile teammate came to them with a newspaper clipping in his hand. He told Sucha and his brother that the police had cracked the case and nabbed the culprits, all from the city of Amritsar.

'What about Jalandhar?' Sucha asked.

'There is no mention of any other district!' replied his brother, after running his gaze through the paragraphs of the clipping.

'How could the police say that it has cracked the case? My kidney was removed in Jalandhar and the racket might still be running there. All of these bastards should be caught before the police claims anything,' Sucha said in an enraged tone.

'The new SP of Amritsar seems to be daring, contrary to the ones where we went to complain and they sent us back, unheard,' Sucha's brother said.

'Should we go to him once? If he is as honest and daring as mentioned in the article, he might hear us out,' Sucha said. His teammate, who was a spectator to this discussion, nodded.

'But I don't think Bapu will allow us. He is already very annoyed with the police department,' his brother said.

'It's not necessary we tell him,' Sucha said and winked. 'I know you can manage something with the help of your sharp mind.'

The next day, Sucha, along with his brother, Sarvan, set out on a journey to Amritsar. Sarvan had convinced his father for a visit to the Golden Temple. It would be good for Sucha's mood, he had said, and luckily, his father had agreed.

Upon reaching Amritsar by bus, they straightaway went to the SP's office, where they were asked to wait for some time as Partap was busy in a meeting. When the PA to SP asked them the reason, Sarvan mentioned something related to land dispute. In case of any other SP, people like Sucha and Sarvan would have been directed to report to the grievance department in the local police station and follow proper channel, but Partap Singh had directed his staff to allow people to meet him on designated days. Luckily for Sucha and Sarvan, it was one of those days.

After waiting for two hours, they were sent into the common room of SP's office building. After another few minutes, Partap called them inside. When he asked them the purpose of their visit, Sucha poured out everything that had happened with him in the recent past. He showed him his old photograph from the days when he was a champion hockey player. Sucha didn't fail to mention that his hair was trimmed and religion was changed on documents before presenting them to the authorisation committee. Sucha's story enraged Partap, but he kept his calm.

'Why didn't you approach the police earlier? And why have you come to me all the way from Ludhiana?' he asked.

'Sir ji, I went to the local police station many times, but my cries fell on deaf ears. We are poor and these people are powerful. They have their connections everywhere. We have come to you because we read that you have nabbed the offenders,' Sarvan said.

'Though Jalandhar city is not under my jurisdiction, I will try to find a solution to get you justice,' Partap consoled the brothers.

'Thank you so much, sir ji,' Sucha said with folded hands and teary eyes.

'But I need your help. I would require a written complaint with Sucha's signatures. In other words, you will have to submit an affidavit,' Partap said. Partap directed the brothers to meet Manjit Singh and get the affidavit written from him. This would become the first written evidence to strengthen the cause of the investigation. The brothers did as directed.

Sucha's affidavit strengthened Partap's belief, and Manjit and the students' claim, that the racket was not limited to Amritsar. Gurkirat had confirmed about Ludhiana and Sucha Singh's complaint included Jalandhar in it.

Partap spent the next couple of nights connecting the dots. He used his influence to get copies of registration documents of all the places, safe houses, clinics and hospitals which were somehow linked to the scam. Surprisingly, all of them pointed towards Jhakhar Hospital. The registrations were done in the name of certain NGOs and businesses, and each of them were supported by the Jhakhar Hospital trust.

A week after Sucha's meeting with Partap, coincidentally, another person named Rajbir Singh approached him and told him that he was one of the donors whose kidney was removed forcefully. Rajbir Singh was thirty-four years old, a father of three children, who lived in Kirpal Nagar, Amritsar. He had been encouraged by the kidney racket news and had decided to approach Partap Singh directly.

In his statement to the SP, he said that when he was on a regular evening walk in the Company Gardens, a man named Chandu had met him and convinced him to donate his kidney for one lakh rupees. A deal was finalised with Pawan Goel, the alleged recipient of kidney and a resident of Rajasthan. However, as days went by, Rajbir decided against the decision of donating his kidney. Two days after he refused Chandu, he was forcibly taken by Chandu and another man named Raju to a house in Rose Avenue where the members of the Goel family were already staying. He tried to escape, but the sedatives he was being given forcibly were quite strong. A half-conscious Rajbir was then presented before the authorisation committee as Rahul, one of the servants of the Goel family. In the first week of July, his kidney was removed at Jhakhar Hospital. After about ten days, the two accused gave him a sum of 40,000 rupees and threatened him against going to the police.

Partap never expected another fresh written complaint in this case. Though his team hadn't found success previously, the news of the arrests made by them had a positive impact and motivated many donors to approach the SP.

The affidavit submitted by Rajbir Singh was solid proof that Jhakhar Hospital was involved. Two fresh evidences along with clues given by Manjit and his team were enough for Partap to start the investigation, but he had to be cautious this time. He called the previous team of the three police officers and this time, the SHO who had registered the FIR against Ricky Bhatia in Tarn Taran was also made part of it.

On the other hand, the activities of middlemen had once again kickstarted without any fear. Not even in their wildest dreams had they thought that their end was being scripted silently by SP Partap Singh.

Chapter 11

After getting his findings and evidences in order and preparing a detailed preliminary report, Partap headed to meet the SSP to update him about the ongoing kidney scam. He presented before his senior official the recent affidavits of Sucha Singh and Rajbir Singh. SSP, though slightly aware about the situation, was still perplexed to see the complexity of the scam. Without wasting any time, he appreciated Partap when he briefed about the leads he had collected from Manjit and the medical students.

'Sir, I request that this be investigated urgently and immediately,' Partap stated with conviction.

'This should be,' the SSP, Mahendra Kumar Mishra, nodded and said as he shuffled through the pages of the affidavits.

'Sir, shall I go ahead then?' asked Partap.

'You should! And keep updating me,' replied the SSP straightaway. 'Official orders shall follow. You go on!' Partap saluted the SSP and left his office.

After getting permission from the higher authority to investigate the case, Partap immediately held a meeting of his team which now comprised of four members, the fourth one being the SHO of Tarn Taran, Kulwant Janjua, who had registered the FIR against Ricky Bhatia. Kulwant Janjua's transfer orders were rendered ineffective with immediate effect upon Partap's request and the SSP assured that he would stay in Tarn Taran till the completion of the investigation.

Partap's instructions to his team were crisp and to-the-point. The officers were to work undercover and avoid involvement of their subordinates until absolutely necessary. ASI Iqbal Singh and SI Kulwant Janjua were tasked to assist Sucha Singh and Rajbir Singh in getting the sketches made for Chandu, Raju and other men involved, who had interacted with them. The tech savvy Gopal Krishan was assigned the task of finding phone numbers of Chandu and Raju through careful analysis of Call Data Records available with telecom service providers, based on timestamps when calls were made to Rajbir by them, and then tracing those numbers for live location. ASI Sukhjeet Singh, former boxing champion, was placed with Gopal Krishan to assist him in apprehending Chandu and Raju, once their locations would be traced. Clear directions were passed by Partap to keep information of any arrest confidential and it was specifically told not to bring Chandu and Raju to the police station. 'Address of a separate location will be shared once they are arrested,' Partap was clear in his instructions.

The four officers, divided into two teams, got on the assigned tasks without delay. Chandu and Raju, who had stopped visiting the hotspots since arrests made by Partap, had to be found using human intelligence and technical surveillance. Owing to Gopal Krishan's genius, their location was traced within twelve hours. They had been hiding in a busy street inside the old city. The challenge for the team was to apprehend them from the crowded area, without anyone noticing. Sukhjeet's knockout punches helped solve this problem as well when he made the two unconscious in the garb of a street-fight over parking issue and then volunteered in front of the crowd to take them to a clinic.

The two were then taken to a location as told by Partap. It was the same house on the outskirts of Amritsar where Partap's Mama and Mami lived. Blindfolded and handcuffed, Chandu and Raju, both bleeding from their nose, were taken upstairs in the room and were tied in a corner.

Partap set out for the location. Within a few minutes, Iqbal and Kulwant also reached the house. Chandu, who was able to regain some consciousness, couldn't still figure out what had happened with him. He opened his eyes widely at the splash of water on his face. He was scared witless to see Partap, in his uniform pants and a white tee, sitting on a chair in front of him.

'Where have you brought me?' asked a scared Chandu.

'That's not important. What is important is that I want to know all the details of the illegal kidney trade from which bastards like you have made a fortune,' Partap said. A half-conscious Raju heard Partap's words.

'Sir, we are not involved in anything like that,' Chandu wanted to take his chances. Partap looked into his eyes for a couple of seconds and stood up immediately.

'Drop them alive from where you have picked them if they tell you everything. Otherwise drop them dead anywhere. I will take care of everything else,' Partap ordered Sukhjeet and walked out of the room.

Panic took the better of Chandu and Raju when they were dragged towards the car as per the SP's orders. Believing that the SP wasn't bluffing, Chandu and Raju cried and pleaded and finally gave up their silence on assurance that nothing would happen to them. Officers recorded their statements in detail as they told them about their role in the modus operandi of the entire kidney racket.

They mentioned Ricky Bhatia as their boss. Dr Bhasin was not mentioned by either. When Partap and his team got all the details, they analyzed the information. The smart SP was able to figure out that such a big scandal could not be run by Ricky Bhatia alone. More men, men of power and authority, or filthy rich men, had to be involved. He wanted to dig deeper.

'You have a tough task ahead of you tomorrow. Arrest all those who have been mentioned by these two cartoons. All the places should be raided at the same time,' said Partap as they stood at the terrace late in the night, while Chandu and Raju were locked inside the room. A caring Mama and Mami had arranged for dinner on the terrace itself, fondly prepared by them for men who were carrying out a difficult task so meticulously.

'Sir, how can four of us raid all these places simultaneously?' an innocent Sukhjeet Singh asked.

'Tomorrow's actions will not be hidden. Prepare your teams at first light and bash on! Chandu and Raju's statements will act as evidences for the FIR,' replied Partap.

'What to do with these two?' asked Iqbal, tilting his head to a side to point downstairs towards the makeshift lockup room.

'They too will be behind bars tomorrow, when everyone else gets there,' replied Partap. 'Until then, take turns to keep a watch on them.'

***

At the crack of dawn the next day, an FIR was registered. Multiple teams led by handpicked officials were briefed by the SP and raids were conducted simultaneously to nab the offenders on the basis of statements given by Chandu and Raju, along with the affidavits submitted by Sucha and Rajbir.

Evidences provided by Manjit Singh and the students had acted as the guiding beacon for Partap and his team. Police ended up arresting more middlemen and doctors involved in the racket – actual ones this time. The kidney recipient in Rajbir Singh's case – Pawan Goel – was also arrested from a four-star hotel.

The police teams did not face any difficulty in capturing the culprits, except in case of advocates who had prepared fake affidavits. When advocate Ranjan Kumar and his brother Anup Kumar were arrested, the advocate fraternity strongly protested against it. Mostly because they felt that both the advocates had nothing to do with the kidney racket. The Amritsar bar council was not happy with the Police and was rendered irked at the behaviour of the new SP.

Subsequently, the council went on a strike. The fear of other advocates, who had somehow been involved in the whole scam, led them to conspire the protest and reel in Jalandhar Bar council as well. They raised serious objections over the investigation. When the police did not heed to their words, all advocates staged a dharna outside the police station. They demanded release of their advocate brothers. Partap, who didn't want to create any ruckus, called the President of Amritsar district bar association and tried to convince him that both Ranjan and Anup were involved in the kidney racket, but he was just not ready to listen.

'Please don't try to shield the culprits unknowingly,' Partap reasoned.

'A person isn't a culprit until proven in court,' said the adamant president.

'What do you want then?' asked an annoyed Partap.

'We want that both of them should be released immediately,' the president replied.

Partap's patience was being tested. Where the president of the council was demanding the release only to earn brownie points and a chance in the next elections, Partap didn't want to release any of the accused. But at the same time, he didn't want the issue to divert the attention of the media and public from the actual problem.

After a brief moment of silence over the phone, Partap decided to release one of the brothers and retain the other brother, against whom there was more evidence.

A case was registered against Ranjan Kumar and Anup Kumar was set free by the police. Partap managed to convince the president of the bar council, showing them evidences against Ranjan.

Every other suspect was thrown behind bars by the police, including Chandu and Raju. When news of these arrests reached Dr Bhasin, it infuriated him. The information of his sources that Partap would not take any further action in the kidney scandal had turned out to be false. He had never expected such a lightning-fast action by the police. That too without even a hint of the proceedings to anyone in the entire department. A puzzled and sulking Bhasin took out his mobile phone and dialled a number.

'What the hell is happening under your nose? Why didn't you stop everything? And I know you knew this was going to happen. Why didn't you—' Dr Bhasin hadn't even completed when the person on the other end started. 'Relax! There is nothing to worry about. And yes, I was well aware. But you must remain patient. Everything will be fine soon.' Before Bhasin could say anything, the person on the other end hung up.

Slowly, the news of the arrests spread like wild fire. News reporters stormed the SP's office, but were not allowed an audience with the SP, who deliberately avoided it. Manjit congratulated Partap over phone. When Gurkirat, Rahul and Kirti came to know about the development, their excitement knew no bounds.

'Good news, after all!' Kirti exclaimed, deliberately whispering as the trio seated themselves inside the library of the medical college.

'Happy to see you happy,' Rahul said and Kirti smiled.

'Its good news indeed! But don't forget that those people running the scam are quite clever. Let's just pray that Partap doesn't get tricked by them,' Gurkirat said and went back into his notes while Rahul and Kirti continued to chat with each other in whispers.

Manjit Singh's reason to worry was akin to Gurkirat's. He wanted to caution Partap every now and then, but didn't want to come off as an overthinker. He just prayed for things to go in the right direction.

The culprits, when thoroughly interrogated by the police, made many shocking revelations. One of the middlemen confirmed deaths of donors on operation table. Chandu accepted his crime and confessed that he used to lure poor people he would handpick at a tea stall to sell their kidneys. He also told the police how he had cremated bodies of donors by declaring them unclaimed illegally to hide the crime and to save those behind the human organ trade. The police also recovered two pocket diaries from him, in which he had listed at least a hundred persons according to their blood groups. He apparently used to act as middleman for these people to sell blood in city's hospitals.

Every culprit, when asked about their boss, mentioned Chandu, Raju, Tinku or Ricky Bhatia. None of them had met or knew about the involvement of Dr Pawan Bhasin in any way. Some of the confessions revealed the role of the authorisation committee in the kidney scam. It was also revealed that the kidney scam was spread in other cities of Punjab as well. After all the statements were recorded, Partap called his team for a meeting to discuss the future course of action.

'Sir, it is time to interrogate the authorisation committee now,' Iqbal suggested as Partap and the four teammates were seated in the conference room adjacent to his office. It was a small soundproof room, with almost a ten feet long u-shaped table in the middle with chairs rightly placed at adequate intervals along the outer side of the table. The framed photographs of Mahatma Gandhi and Dr B.R. Ambedkar hung on the front wall were the silent onlookers.

'Sir, why don't we arrest the members of the committee?' asked Sukhjeet.

'No,' Partap shook his head thoughtfully. 'We can't arrest them as of now. They are reputed people. It will take solid evidences and more confessions to put them behind bars.'

'What do we do then?' Kulwant asked.

'Issue notice to the authorisation committee chairman to join the investigation. We will make him confess in exchange for immunity,' Partap said.

'Yes sir,' Kulwant replied.

Partap kept updating the SSP about the developments. After a go-ahead from the SSP, a notice was issued to the chairman of the authorisation committee to become part of the investigation. When Chairman Prem Prasad Mahajan saw the notice, he panicked at first and then bluntly refused to accept the offer, citing organisational commitments. Partap never expected this rejection. The haphazard refusal by Prem Prasad indirectly proved his involvement in the scandal, but in order to prove it and interrogate him, Partap needed permission from his seniors. Prasad was, after all, the principal of Medical College and his direct arrest was bound to cause unrest in the city.

Partap called Manjit to his office and updated him with the latest developments. Manjit hailed Partap's efforts, but deep down, he was not satisfied to learn that Partap had not found any evidence against Dr Bhasin yet. The kingpin was still out of the police's reach. Partap also conveyed his inability to straightway arrest or raid the office of the authorisation committee chairman, and Manjit understood his limitations.

'But now that the culprits have admitted that the case files were approved by the authorisation committee, their role in the scam is proved. I don't think any more evidence is required to interrogate Prem Prasad?' Manjit suggested.

'Which is why I am preparing a case file with all evidences to present it to the SSP and then IG for permission to go ahead against the authorisation committee,' said Partap.

No sooner did Manjit leave than Partap, who was compiling the details in a file, received an unexpected call from the IG's office. To his surprise, he was called to the IG's office by the IG himself. He compiled whatever he could find and rushed to Jalandhar in his service vehicle without delay. After reaching the office of the IG and waiting for a few minutes, IG Akash Gupta called him inside his office.

'So here comes the best officer of the department,' IG exclaimed joyfully as he got up from his chair. 'Have a seat!'

'Thank you, sir,' Partap stamped his right foot and saluted and then seated himself. The IG ran his fingers in his grey hair groomed in a crew cut style, opened a box of Dunhill cigarettes, pulled one out and lit it with a classic zippo lighter. Before he talked any further, he took a long puff of smoke which shrouded his oval, weather-beaten yet clean shaven face for a moment. His small eyes further narrowed by wrinkles on the sides were however fixed at Partap all this while. Partap, quite junior to the IG in both rank and service, felt uneasy at this judgemental glance. It was the first time he was meeting him in person.

'You did a good job, Partap! But you failed to follow my instructions,' the IG said.

'How… sir?' Partap asked, hesitantly.

'I asked you to keep any investigation related to the kidney scam a secret between you and me only. Were my orders ambiguous?' asked the IG, still puffing smoke calmly.

'Sir, preliminary investigation was carried out secretly, but we had to go all out in order to nab the culprits who worked at a higher level of hierarchy in this scam,' Partap said in his efforts to justify, without sounding defiant.

'But I wasn't updated,' the IG said, embarrassing Partap. 'Relax! I've not called you here to discipline you. You did a good job already. But I still wish you had heeded my words,' Akash Gupta said.

'Sir, your words are very important to me and I wanted to gather all information before updating you. But before I could come to you, you called me yourself,' Partap said and forwarded a file to the IG.

'What is this?' asked Gupta.

'Sir, this file contains all the evidences and statements of offenders in which they have accepted their crime and revealed the modus operandi of the entire kidney scam. It is clear from all the information that the authorisation committee is also involved in the scandal. I had sent a notice to the chairman of the committee to join the investigation, but he bluntly refused,' a proud Partap said while IG shuffled through the pages of the file with a burning cigarette in his mouth leaving strands of smoke up in the air.

'Hmmm.'

'Sir, my team has done all the homework. Now we seek your permission to move further with the investigation and unearth the whole scandal. I am sure some influential people are involved in it. But first of all, we need to interrogate the chairman,' said Partap.

Akash Gupta did not utter a word in reply. He kept on reading through the pages of the file with his head buried into the pages. The butt of a long-extinguished cigarette still remained between his lips. After a couple of minutes, he closed the file, threw the butt of the cigarette in the ash tray and sat back in his chair with the file in his lap.

'Let me go through all the details thoroughly. Then I will see what to do next,' said the IG.

'Right, sir!' Partap said.

'You have done a great job, but don't think that this will save you from my wrath for disobeying my orders,' Akash Gupta said and grinned.

A confused Partap, who couldn't make out if it was a pun, remained silent, got out of the chair, saluted the IG and walked out of his office. All he was now left to do was to wait for further orders from IG Akash Gupta.

Partap also wasn't able to figure out what 'wrath' he would face. Lost in the thoughts, he went home early that day. He could not sleep all night. The next day, when he was sitting in his office, he received a call from the SSP, who wanted to see him immediately. Partap rushed to his office. A news awaited him there.

The SSP informed him that the case of the kidney scam has been shifted to the vigilance bureau (VB). Partap was puzzled. He had been working on the case with all the sincerity and had put all his efforts. This sudden transfer of the case was beyond his comprehension.

The SSP was speechless because the orders had come from above. A depressed Partap left his office in a state of shock. Firstly, he thought that this could be the 'wrath' IG had sarcastically mentioned about. But when he pondered over it, he understood that it could not be the case. He kept on joining the pieces of the puzzle and came to a shocking conclusion – what if IG Akash Gupta was trying to protect the actual culprits!

His words of keeping the investigation a secret and his act of keeping the file containing all the vital information were the things which Partap should have noticed at that time only. Transfer of case to the Crime Branch and VB was the most efficient method of hushing it up. When Manjit Singh and the students learned about these latest developments, they were left disappointed. Manjit tried to dig deeper and found out from one of his sources who was a travel agent that

IG Akash Gupta and Dr Pawan Bhasin were close friends and often went on foreign trips together.

He immediately called Partap and informed him about the same.

'My conclusion was on point then,' Partap said disappointedly.

'Indeed!' Manjit replied.

'And the worst part is that the master file containing all the statements and evidences is with the IG,' Partap said dejectedly, as realization dawned on him.

'We have lost everything… again,' Manjit stated. Partap remained silent and hung up.

***

A wide steel gate opened and a white Mercedes Benz made way through it as it sped up on a road surrounded by lush green gardens on both sides before stopping in front of a farm house located on the outskirts of Amritsar. IG Akash Gupta, dressed in white tracks sporting a red cap stepped out of the car with his golf kit and entered the front porch of the exquisite building. He was welcomed with a warm hug by Dr Pawan Bhasin, who was dressed for a golf session. Both of them went inside and straight towards the bar counter.

'A friend in need is a friend indeed!' Dr Bhasin patted Gupta's shoulder and exclaimed joyfully.

'Thank you,' replied the IG.

'But this time, I was quite worried that you would be late,' said the doctor.

'It was required, Doc.'

'Why?' asked Bhasin.

'To make you realize that I will not be the IG forever, who will come to the rescue every time. Sometimes, you have to deal with things on your own. I acted late just because I wanted that the loopholes in your trade get exposed,' replied the IG. 'Now that we know about all of them, you work on fixing them and enjoy your business.'

'How clever and mindful of you!' Bhasin said as the two clung their whiskey glasses together. 'But what if that Partap Singh had reached us?'

'I had my eyes on him. I let him reach your stupid dumb friend, that Chairman Prem Prasad Mahajan,' the IG replied with a cunning laugh. 'I just like to see that coward wet his pants.' Gupta joined the IG in his laughter.

In the coming days, to Partap's bad luck, all the apprehended suspects turned hostile in court. They stated that the police had tried to put words into their mouth forcefully. Lack of further evidences against them weakened the individual cases against each of the suspects and they were eventually released on bail. Manjit Singh, the students and Partap remained silent spectators.

Dr Bhasin halted his activities and instructed his staff to work on the loopholes. The charges against Ricky Bhatia and Tinku were dropped and they were called back from Nepal to join Dr Bhasin's gang once again.

Chapter 12

Manjit Singh opened the door quickly upon incessant ringing of the bell. It was Gurkirat, Kirti and Rahul. The students, depressed at the news of transfer of the case from Partap to VB, wanted to meet Manjit to understand the situation.

'Do we consider that they've won again?' Gurkirat asked in a low, melancholic tone.

'I guess so,' replied Manjit, avoiding eye contact with anyone.

'If an SP couldn't reach to the bottom of it, how do we hope anyone can?' Kirti said.

'This time, we actually had many hopes, but all shattered now,' a frustrated Rahul said before cursing in Bhojpuri.

Manjit listened to the whining students as they kept on talking about how unjust the system had become that even an SP couldn't do anything about the kidney scam. He stared at their faces, only to realise how heartbroken the young souls were.

'Don't lose hope,' Manjit said. 'Nothing is shattered yet. We will continue fighting till the culprits are brought to justice.'

'But how is fighting even possible anymore?' Gurkirat asked. He noticed Manjit's health was slowly improving. The bruises on his face had long gone. His skin color was back to normal. But his body was still weak and he needed support to sit or stand.

'We will find a way as we have always done. So what if Partap is not handling this case anymore! He is still an honest SP who can help us in many ways,' said Manjit in an attempt to motivate the students.

'But I don't see a way,' Gurkirat said.

'I too see all the doors closed now,' said a depressed Rahul.

'When some doors close, others open. We just have to be watchful enough to find them,' Manjit said.

'I think I have found one,' Kirti, who had been thinking hard for a while, said all of a sudden.

'And that would be?' Gurkirat asked.

'We have to start a movement now. Let a wave of angered public protests build pressure on the current government,' Kirti suggested. 'And for that to happen, we should go to the press.'

'Press… media… local journalists to cover the news and spread it to all households,' Gurkirat added.

'Exactly!' Kirti reacted excitedly.

'The idea is… a revolutionary one, but I don't think we will be able to find any press correspondents to help us at this time,' Gurkirat said. 'Baljit Rana, the only one who tried to help us the last time received threats and was almost fired by his editor-in-chief.' Gurkirat's words slayed Kirti's excitement in a jiffy.

Manjit, who was listening to the conversation, was silently busy weighing the pros and cons of Kirti's suggestion.

'Chachaji, what is your opinion on this?' Gurkirat asked Manjit.

'In the current situation, I think this is the best solution we have. Public has the power to overthrow anything, even when everything else fails. It all depends on how to incite them,' he replied. 'I am sure fearless, bold and matter-of-fact reporting can help us here.'

'Hey, why don't you talk to your brother who gave us the reference of Baljit Rana?' Kirti asked Gurkirat.

'You know he is not in Amritsar,' replied Gurkirat.

'So what? This racket is no longer confined to Amritsar, Punjab or even India. A story can be published from anywhere,' Manjit said.

'Bhaiya is right. The story is important at this point of time, doesn't matter if it is published from Amritsar or anywhere else,' added Kirti.

'You're a genius!' Rahul playfully hit Kirti with a cushion. She nodded and winked back at him. Gurkirat and Manjit exchanged curious looks for a moment.

'Okay. I will call my cousin today and try to convince him,' Gurkirat replied.

'You establish contact with your cousin. Meanwhile, Rahul and I will go meet Baljit Rana today. If he also agrees, it will impact harder,' Manjit said.

'I'm just worried...' Rahul said, 'could this be our last resort? What if this too doesn't work?'

Manjit patted on Rahul's shoulder and said, '*Rabb Rakha* (god be the saviour).'

Gurkirat called his cousin who now published his own newspaper, though with scarce circulation. He asked him to publish a story on Partap Singh and tell the public how an honest officer was removed from the case just to save the culprits. Gurkirat's cousin, who initially didn't agree, was later convinced by Gurkirat using emotional blackmail as he cited examples of how poor people were cheated and how journalism was an important pillar in democracy. Gurkirat's cousin demanded two days' time to develop the news.

Manjit and Rahul went to Baljit Rana's office later that day and asked him to help them once again, but Baljit had a different story to tell them.

'My editor-in-chief will never allow this. You know very well what had happened last time. I almost lost my job,' Baljit Rana was straightforward in his reply.

'You should talk to him once,' Manjit tried to convince.

'It is of no use. He will never agree,' Baljit replied.

'Can you take me to him? Let me talk to him once,' asked Manjit.

'It is futile. I am telling you he won't agree,' Baljit replied, louder this time.

'Please,' Manjit folded his hands and bent forward. 'Just take me to his office once.'

After about half an hour, Manjit was sitting in the editor-in-chief's office, along with Rahul and Baljit Rana. When Manjit requested him to publish the story, he straightaway refused. He told Manjit everything that had happened with him previously, and he said he didn't want to indulge in the whole kidney scam again.

'I have faced trauma as well,' Manjit said, stood up, turned to a side and tugged at his shirt to show the incision scar from the surgery. 'Just a little more than yours.'

'What is this?' the editor asked as he narrowed his gaze to look at the scar on Manjit's torso.

'This is what has happened to hundreds of poor people against their wish. They were duped, abused and some of them were also killed by the culprits,' said Manjit. 'Their only hope was SP Partap Singh, who could have delivered them justice. But his hands have been tied as well.'

A curious air of silence filled the room. The editor-in-chief sat back in his chair, contemplating. He was clearly facing a dilemma; Manjit could tell from the expressions on his face. He wanted to side with the innocent, but he still feared the culprits. Baljit Rana tried to convince his boss, but he didn't break his silence. A couple minutes later, Manjit Singh got up from his chair. Rahul followed him. They looked towards each other with dissatisfaction.

'It was nice meeting you, Joshi ji. I had only come here to see how you've been keeping up with the hundred-years-old legacy of your newspaper, which claims to spread the truth,' Manjit Singh said with folded hands and then quietly left the office with Rahul, while Baljit kept sitting there. After a few minutes, the editor got up from his chair and left his office, without exchanging any words with Baljit.

Manjit Singh and the students were satisfied when two days later, a cover story related to Partap Singh was published by Gurkirat's cousin in his newspaper. Though the circulation of that paper wasn't up to the mark, it grabbed the general public attention. Gurkirat called his cousin and told him to continue publishing the stories related to donors to spread the word. His strategy worked and after a couple of days, where the news about kidney scam started spreading among the public, the newspaper's subscription saw a gradual rise.

One morning, Baljit Rana received an early morning call from his editor-in-chief, who was at Amritsar airport.

'I am going to London for some official work and I'm leaving you in charge of the Sunday special edition,' he said. After a brief pause, he continued. 'And remember, the truth must come out.'

Baljit was smart enough to understand the underlying hint. He immediately got up and started working on his story. The next day it was published as the cover story of Sunday's edition of the newspaper. Baljit was courageous enough to frame the headline which questioned the government about Partap's removal in the kidney scam case. It went like '*The last hope of hundreds wronged in the infamous Kidney Scam side-lined. Why is the government shielding the illegal organ traders?*'

In the coming days, he published more stories about the scam in the regular newspaper. Other small-scale news agencies republished similar news, and in no time, simultaneous revelations by multiple newspapers started getting traction to the kidney scam news. More and more people, in Amritsar as well as in other cities of Punjab, began to get aware of the scam. A wave of public unrest, which the students and Manjit Singh had dreamt of, had started to take shape. Within a few days, the kidney scam became the talk of the town and many NGOs came forward in support of the victims. Where Nirmala Devi, the opposition leader slammed the government, the other leader, Harpal Dang demanded a CBI enquiry in this regard.

Dr Bhasin tore the newspaper in rage, which contained the story related to the kidney scam. He immediately called his associates for a meeting and instructed them to 'take care' of the reporters. Within no time, goons headed by Ricky Bhatia thronged Baljit Rana's office. Luckily, he was not there. They started hunting for him.

Baljit, unaware of any developments, had gone to the Golden Temple to pay his obeisance. When he came back, he was frightened to learn that the goons had thrashed everything in his office and were looking for him. He immediately called Manjit and informed him about Dr Bhasin's intentions.

Manjit wasted no time to go to Partap Singh to seek his support. The SP, sensing the gravity of the matter, immediately gave security cover to Baljit Rana. The reporter continued receiving threats afterwards as well, but as Partap's support filled more courage in him, he didn't give an ear to them.

Manjit's far-sightedness also helped in saving the life of Gurkirat's cousin on whom an attack was planned. The retired advocate, with Partap's help, had got police protection for Gurkirat's cousin in advance, which had kept the goons at bay. Both Baljit Rana and Gurkirat's cousin were rendered more fearless in publishing stories to fetch justice for the poor – all thanks to the police support backed by Partap.

Baljit kept marching ahead fearlessly and procured some vital evidences through his sources in connection with Dr Bhasin and IG Gupta.

'I have got some copies of personal photographs of Bhasin, which show how close the IG and Bhasin are,' he said to Manjit Singh over a phone call.

'So, this only confirms what my sources had told me,' replied Manjit.

'I have also got documents which reveal that these two often spend their holidays together abroad,' Baljit Rana said.

'It's good that we have documents now. Keep them safe; we will need them later,' Manjit said and hung up the phone.

He immediately called Pratap. The whole revelation made it clear that it had been Dr Bhasin behind the whole kidney scam all this while.

Dr Bhasin, on the other hand, felt helpless for the first time. Media coverage wasn't something he feared earlier. IG Gupta asked him to lie low for a while. Even though Bhasin agreed, but the devil inside him kept on sulking within. The only thing he could think of was revenge. He wasn't going to let the reporter get away so easily. Years of hard work in building a reputation would not be wiped away by a mere reporter, he decided. When the sulking reached a point where he couldn't deal with it anymore, Bhasin ordered his associates to kill Baljit Rana. All he had to do was to make a deal with police personnel deployed for Rana's protection. When things fell in place, Rana's fate was sealed.

At around ten one morning, when Baljit was getting ready for office, eight men with their faces covered with cloth and makeshift masks, barged into his room and attacked him with sharp-edged weapons. Baljit was so shocked that he couldn't even resist. The injured reporter, with his body criss-crossed with sharp cuts at various places, somehow managed to run out of his home. The hitmen followed him. He was petrified to see that the police personnel who were designated to guard his house were not there.

Mustering all the leftover energy, Baljit stumbled along the narrow lane towards the market, shouting for help. None of the spectators came forward.

The goons walked behind him, fearlessly brandishing their weapons. The pedestrians changed directions and sped away from the scene. Baljit's off-white shirt was crimson as he now crawled on the cemented road. The goons circled around him when he couldn't crawl anymore. Unable to talk anymore, Baljit lifted his trembling, blood-stained hand to gesture them to stop as he sat against the shutter of a closed shop with his almost lifeless body drenched in blood. He breathed heavily and his vision faded. His neighbours peered from the parapets of their houses. Some of them closed their windows. A very old turbaned rickshaw puller came forward to plead to the goons, but was kicked away ruthlessly. Nobody else dared to utter a word.

One of the eight men stepped forward towards Baljit, cupped his chin in his hand and slowly, effortlessly, pushed the sharp knife into his throat. Baljit gagged for a while, choking on his blood, and then his lifeless head dropped to a side. The men vanished in different directions towards different narrow lanes.

Manjit Singh, who was on his way to Baljit's house to get evidences, saw a crowd gathered in the market and went towards it. He was taken aback to see Baljit Rana's blood-stained body lying in a pool of blood. A seemingly shocked Manjit pulled himself back together and looked for the police personnel. Finding none, he asked the onlookers to step away from the dead body and called Partap on his mobile phone.

In hardly any time, Partap rushed to the spot with an ambulance. The nurse checked Baljit's pulse and disclosed that the reporter was already dead. Partap and Manjit questioned the crowd present there for any witnesses. The crowd started to disperse.

Partap and Manjit knew very well that this was planned by Dr Bhasin's goons, but they had no evidence. When they were about walk away, a middle-aged man came running towards them with a handycam.

'Sir, this handycam contains the visuals of the murder,' he said to Partap.

'Who are you?' Manjit asked.

'I am just a cameraman who was hired to record the marriage ceremony two blocks away. When I saw some men attacking a person in the background, I secretly recorded everything. I am really sorry I couldn't help him,' the man said.

Partap took the handycam from him and thanked him for his presence of mind. Baljit's dead body was taken away by the ambulance.

A heartbroken Manjit pleaded the SP to find the goons and bring them to justice. Pratap was both grieving and enraged, and promised Manjit that quick action would be taken.

Later that day, Manjit suggested that Partap should give parts of the footage to media channels to garner public sympathy. Partap did as suggested and their efforts paid off.

Dr Bhasin had no idea know that Baljit Rana's murder would act as the final nail in his coffin.

When the news channels played the tape on air and linked it to the news of the kidney scam, a wave of mass unrest erupted. All press and media were enraged by the incident, which had left a reporter dead in broad daylight. As a result, their reporting of the illegal kidney trade intensified. People condemned the barbaric murder everywhere. In the coming days, a plethora of human rights organisations and NGOs came forward and condemned the macabre murder of the reporter.

'We should also go and join the protest,' Kirti said to her friends in the empty classroom post the lecture.

'Baljit bhaiya was a fearless man, true to his profession,' Gurkirat said in a sad tone. 'We should have seen this coming. If those goons could threaten us, it was only natural they would have planned worse things for someone who was busting them. Things are out in the open now and I fear if we join the protest, we might be attacked too.'

'We can't sit idle and watch the show,' Kirti said in an irritable tone. 'Baljit bhaiya's sacrifice should not go in vain.'

'I think we have done enough already,' a worried Rahul said.

'Our job is incomplete till the mastermind is captured,' Kirti retorted.

'What else can we do then?' Gurkirat asked.

'Youth power,' Kirti said. 'It is time to show what youth can achieve. Let us go to the head of the students union and ask him to join the protest with other students. I am sure he will agree.'

'Why will he do that?' Rahul asked.

'Because we will convince him that due to a few bad people, the reputation of doctors is getting maligned. If the culprits don't get caught, it will further worsen the scenario and no one will trust us,' Kirti replied. 'Besides, he will have to agree for his image. Student elections are round the corner. Protesting for something good will make him likeable, you see.'

'Good idea,' Gurkirat commented. 'And if other students will join the protest, our parents won't have a problem with us joining the same.'

'Exactly!' Kirti said and got up from her seat.

The trio went to the president of the students union and somehow convinced him to plan the protests. Kirti played with her words well. She even suggested getting billboards and posters printed. Things went as planned and a protest was called by the students union soon after. It started inside the college premises and was joined by hundreds of students. Later, someone suggested that other colleges should be pulled into the protest as well.

The students union president called the student leaders of other medical colleges of Punjab and convinced them to join the protest. Soon, thousands of students came onto the roads to protest against the kidney scam. Hundreds of freelance reporters joined them with posters of Baljit Rana in their hands. The SP designated roads for a peaceful protest and arranged for re-routing of the traffic from such roads.

Kirti, Rahul and Gurkirat, along with other leaders, led the protest from the front in Amritsar. Similar protests on the same days, and similar times were organised in cities like Jalandhar, Ludhiana, Bathinda and Chandigarh. Nationwide media covered the protests. Regular candle-marches became the hot topic. Where Manjit Singh was delighted to see the power of the youth, Dr Bhasin and his associates bit their fingernails.

The principal of the Medical College and the chairman of authorisation committee, Dr Prem Prasad Mahajan, tried to stop the students a couple of times, but the protests had reached a scale where nobody listened to him anymore. Along with all this, the leaders of the opposition parties started reprimanding the current government in the legislative assembly. This inflated the worries of Dr Bhasin and he made a frantic call to the IG.

'I can't remain quiet anymore. You must do something now,' said the doctor.

'Who asked you to kill that reporter? How could you be so stupid, Bhasin? I thought doctors were intelligent people,' Gupta lashed at Bhasin over phone. 'I had specifically instructed you to lie low for some time, but you spoiled everything. Anyway, I will still do one last thing for you when the time comes. But for now, remove all traces of your illegal work from everywhere.'

'Hahaha,' Bhasin let out a mocking laugh and said, 'All that is left of the powerful inspector general of police is advices?'

'One wrong move by us at this time will put us in a serious situation. I can lose my job. I am already on the receiving end of criticism for shifting the case to VB,' Gupta replied.

'Why don't you put everyone behind bars?' Dr Bhasin said in frustration.

'Talk sense, Bhasin. How can I jail thousands of people? Let everything cool down and then we will recover. Goodbye for now,' said the IG and hung up the phone. Dr Bhasin smashed the receiver on the floor in anger.

A convoy of white ambassador cars marched out of the Chandigarh airport premises. The Chief Minister, Arvinder Singh, was back in the state after participating in an election campaign in Gujarat for days. Within a few minutes of resuming his office, he called the ADGP cum OSD, Saqib Ahmed for an emergency meeting.

'Why was this case of kidney scam transferred to VB without my consent?' the CM asked the ADGP.

Two old men, men of power and authority, both honest towards their respective professions, spoke for the first time on the kidney scam.

'Sir, this was done by IG Akash Gupta unanimously,' Saqib said. There was a look of mutual frustration on both faces. One man's unanimous decision had set a lot of wrong things in motion and both the CM and ADGP's facial expressions acknowledged the same. Both, however, were wise enough to not let frustration get the better of them.

'The damage is done,' the turbaned CM, Arvinder Singh, said as he adjusted his reading glasses. 'Make amends immediately.'

'Yes sir,' the ADGP replied firmly.

'I want you to form a special investigation team (SIT) in this regard and shift the case to it. You will personally head the team. I want you to thoroughly probe the racket and bring it to a logical conclusion.' the CM said as he read through a couple of files piled up in his 'in' tray on the desk.

'It will be done, sir,' Saqib said, lifting his service cap resting calmly in his lap to wear it. The ADGP got up, saluted the CM still busy reading the files, and left.

After the meeting, the CM immediately issued orders for the transfer of IG Akash Gupta. This move of the chief minister was welcomed by the press and media. The transfer of the case back to the police department was hailed by the press as an effort on the part of the chief minister to ensure 'free and fair' investigation. The students and Manjit Singh were elated by the decision. The mass movement against the kidney scam was working. It was sad someone had to die for it.

Saqib Ahmad, as told by the CM, called Raman Sharma, IPS, IGP, Jalandhar zone to form a SIT. The IGP then constituted the team of police officers comprising Partap Singh, SP City,

Amritsar; Gurjant Singh, PPS, the SP HQs, Hoshiarpur; and Ranjodh Singh, PPS, DSP, staff officer to IGP, Jalandhar zone. The four officers in Partap's team were also kept in the special investigation team on Partap's recommendation. Saqib Ahmed ordered that the range DIGs would verify the kidney donation files relating to their areas of jurisdiction and report the discrepancies to the SIT.

The students and Manjit Singh congratulated Partap Singh on getting the case back. Where the news of formation of a special investigation team and transfer of IG Gupta was welcomed by NGOs and opposition leaders, it wreaked havoc on Dr Bhasin and other perpetrators. He called all his contacts, including his politician friends, for help, but no one paid heed to his words this time. Nobody wanted to get involved in anything now.

Later that night, Dr Bhasin received an SMS on his mobile phone. He immediately got up, sat in his car and drove to the location specified in the message. IG Gupta was standing there, alone. He wanted to meet Dr Bhasin once before leaving his current office.

'How is golf practice going on, doc?' Gupta asked.

'Have you called me here to ask these silly questions?' Dr Bhasin retorted annoyingly.

'Of course not. I just wanted to see my friend once,' said the IG with a visible smile as the car's light fell on his face. Bhasin nodded in annoyance.

'Don't be upset! Everything will be fine soon,' Gupta said.

'An SIT has been formed, you have been transferred and no other person is ready to help me. You still think everything will be fine? What a joke!' replied Dr Bhasin in anger.

'They will find nothing,' IG Gupta said.

'What do you mean?' Dr Bhasin asked.

'They will find nothing, because I have destroyed the only original case file of the kidney scam that Partap had prepared. It included all the evidences and statements of people arrested by him. Without that, it would be almost impossible for him to proceed further. All you have to do is to send all these people underground till the enquiry is finished,' replied Gupta.

'You...' Bhasin's expression changed into a relieving one, 'You did it already? I am speechless. Thank you, Gupta.'

'I have played my part one last time. Now it's upon you to handle it from here on. As I had told you earlier also, do not leave a single trace in any of your establishments of what you had been doing,' Gupta said.

'You have saved me once again. You're my true friend,' Dr Bhasin said and embraced the IG in his arms.

IG Gupta's assurance gave strength to a depressed Dr Bhasin.

The very next morning, he went to check himself, whether his orders for removal of all the traces related to kidney trade were followed by his staff or not. After a thorough check, he heaved a sigh of relief and ordered all his associates to go underground for the time being.

In the coming days, range DIGs verified a total of 2055 files of kidney donations and presented their findings to OSD Saqib Ahmad and SIT. The data was astonishing. The DIG of Jalandhar range said that he had verified 611 files of donors and found out that out of those, 59 were genuine donors and remaining 552 were not genuine.

The DIG of Ludhiana range verified 450 files in total and found out that 256 were genuine donors while 194 were orchestrated.

The DIG Border range reported that he had gone through 519 files and concluded that only 26 were genuine donors.

The Patiala range DIG said that he had gone through 312 files of donors in total and found out that only 66 donors were genuine out of those.

DIG Ferozepur reported that only 54 donors were genuine out of 99 files he had examined.

Lastly, DIG Faridkot range reported that he had only found 20 genuine donors in the 64 files he had examined.

'The data is really surprising,' Saqib Ahmad said in a meeting of the range DIGs in Chandigarh.

'Sir, this data is from 28 March 1997, till date. The kidney trades are happening since almost five years,' one of the DIGs said.

'It means that this trade flourished in the tenure of the previous government. Maybe the kingpin was hand in the glove with the leaders who must have also benefitted from the trade,' said Saqib. 'This data is really disturbing. I will discuss everything with the Chief Minister.'

It was clear from the preliminary investigation that many people from all across Punjab were involved in it. At first, criminal cases were registered against all the donors and recipients involved in fake cases by the police. Though later, no action was taken on those on humanitarian grounds, because the government officials at the highest level felt that recipients needed the transplants in order to save their lives, and the donors gave away the organ to earn basic livelihood.

The recipients were forced for their need to survive, which compelled them to enter into a monetary deal with doctors and middlemen. The donors, on the other hand, were those people who could not even make both ends meet and were ready to sell organs to earn a living. They were only given a meagre amount of the rich booty earned by the doctors and middlemen. It was actually the middlemen and doctors who were the real culprits. Apart from this, the recipients and donors who were traced through their files by the DIGs, survived on a heavy dose of medication and battled with their life already. It wouldn't do anyone any good to pursue all the cases.

'We need to keep our focus on the doctors and the middlemen involved in this illicit trade,' Saqib Ahmad told the SIT in a meeting in Jalandhar. 'Hunt down the suspects and bring everyone to justice. I am giving you a free hand.'

'Just what was required, sir. Thank you,' Partap Singh said.

'I want results. This kidney racket should be uprooted from its roots,' Saqib said.

'Yes sir,' everyone replied in unison.

After giving instructions, the OSD stomped out of the room. His words filled courage in Partap and his team. The SP and other members of the SIT were now ready to go to war against the culprits. Manjit Singh and the students prayed for Partap's success this time.

Chapter 13

Sucha Singh's mother gazed at the old wall clock hung on the lobby wall. It was half past nine in the night and dinner was ready. She desperately waited for Sucha, who would go to the hockey ground regularly in the evening and would usually return by seven. It was two-and-a-half hours past his usual time of return and each passing minute only increased her heart rate. After a few minutes, there was a knock at the door and she ran towards it. When she opened the door, Sucha's father pushed his bicycle inside the house.

'It was a tiring day,' he said as he put the bicycle on stand in the verandah. 'I am starving. Is dinner ready?'

'Yes, it is ready, but Sucha hasn't come back yet,' his wife replied in a worried tone.

'What? Where is he?' asked Sucha's father.

'He went to the ground like every day, but hasn't returned yet. He has never stayed out for so long. I am really worried now,' replied Sucha's mother as she paced up and down near the bicycle. 'You should go and enquire about him.'

'I am going, don't worry,' Sucha's father said as he took the bicycle off the stand and rushed out of the main door. He cycled through the badly-lit narrow bricked lanes of the village and went to the hockey ground in search of Sucha. As expected, he didn't find anyone there, except a few stray gs. Anxiety took over him and he quickly paddled his cycle owards the house one of Sucha's friends.

'Is Sucha at your home?' he asked when Sucha's friend opened the gate.

'No, uncle, what happened?' Sucha's friend asked.

'Your friend hasn't reached home yet,' a worried father replied.

'He was with me in the evening and we left the ground together. In fact, I had dropped him just a few yards away from your house,' the boy said with conviction.

'But he didn't come home,' the old man said, almost to himself.

'It's strange,' Sucha's friend said. 'Where else could he be?'

'Please do me a favour, son. Enquire about Sucha from all your friends while I go to some other places in search of him,' Sucha's father said and cycled away.

He searched every corner and went through every street of the village, asking some of the people, but there was no clue of Sucha. Sucha's friends also started searching for him in a group. They went to all the probable places where Sucha could go, but didn't find any trace. At around midnight, they went to Sucha's house to inform his father. Upon knowing that her son was nowhere to be found, Sucha's mother burst into tears. She, as well as others, feared the worst.

'He must have tried to harm himself,' his father said in a low voice and his words were enough to further weaken the hopes of Sucha's mother, who sat on the floor, already crying uncontrollably.

'He can't do any such thing. I know him well. He is very happy now,' one of Sucha's friends said. 'You need not worry.

We will lodge a complaint in the police station tomorrow morning, and they will find him for sure.'

At the crack of dawn, Sucha's parents and his friends, who had hardly slept all night, went along with the Sarpanch of the village to the local police station and lodged a complaint with respect to Sucha's disappearance.

On the same day, another complaint was filed in Amritsar's B division police station. It was about the mysterious disappearance of Rajbir Singh, the victim of kidney scam who had earlier submitted his affidavit to Partap Singh. In her statement to the police, his wife said that Rajbir had been missing since the previous night. He had gone to fetch an LPG cylinder from a neighbour, but did not return. She, along with her three young children, searched for him all night long, but didn't get any clue. All relatives and friends of Rajbir Singh were also unaware of his whereabouts.

Immediately after registering the complaint, ill thoughts flooded her mind and she fainted at the police station. She was rushed to the nearby hospital where she regained consciousness after about an hour.

'Where is my husband?' Rajbir's wife enquired just as she woke up, drained of all energy due to her worries.

'He will come back, don't worry. Just take rest,' one of her relatives assured her.

'Where are my children?' she quickly asked the second question.

'They are safe at our home,' the relative replied.

Though Rajbir's wife was given assurance by her relatives, she started crying and tried to get up from the bed.

When her relatives were unable to handle her, they called the doctor who gave her sedatives so that she could rest. The police was quick to launch its investigation upon receiving complaints regarding Sucha and Rajbir. These two men being the prime witnesses were important to the investigation. Therefore, news about their disappearance had reached SIT in no time. Search parties were sent out. Roadblocks were established closer to their areas and vehicles were checked. Photographs of the two were faxed across all the police stations of Punjab.

Despite their best efforts, the police was unable to trace Sucha and Rajbir anywhere in the state in the next twenty-four hours. Each passing minute filled more tension in the families of the two poor kidney scam victims.

The officers of the SIT were on their toes. They were leaving no stone unturned in search of the culprits and related evidences. Regular raids were being conducted at various places. The employees, including doctors of the blood bank and Jhakhar Hospital were being questioned. Similar raids were conducted at suspected hospitals in Ludhiana and Jalandhar. Every file, every record was searched for discrepancies. Partap Singh also wanted to question the advocates who had prepared affidavits of ingenuine cases found by range DIGs, but the government's decision to not pursue any case against donors and recipients and not to involve them in any enquiry hampered his plan. Moreover, to pursue investigation against advocates on the basis of files, he required fresh statements of donors and he was unsure about their cooperation. Sucha and Rajbir had themselves walked up to Partap before the government took the decision.

After every raid, members of the team held meetings with Raman Sharma to discuss the current situation, who then updated Saqib Ahmad.

'What's the progress so far?' Sharma, senior among the team of officers, asked the other SPs.

'Sir, we are regularly conducting raids, but nothing has been found yet,' Partap replied.

'Sir, it appears that the culprits have erased every record,' Gurjant Singh said.

'I also think so,' said Ranjodh Singh. 'We are unable to find anything because it has been replaced or done away with.'

'What about those who were arrested earlier and later released?' Sharma asked Partap.

'Sir, almost all of them have run away. We couldn't trace any of them. Only the advocate brothers are there, but we don't have any evidence against them now. The only evidence, the affidavits of Sucha Singh and Rajbir Singh, went away with the file which I had handed over to IG Akash Gupta. And by questioning them without proper evidence, we may invite wrath of the advocate community again,' Partap replied. 'That file is really important, sir, because it contains all the evidences against all the culprits.'

'I will request Saqib sir to get that file from IG. But why don't you get fresh affidavits from Sucha and Rajbir?' Raman Sharma asked.

'We are searching them, sir!' Partap replied while others preferred to stay quiet, sensing that Raman Sharma had not been informed about the disappearances.

'What do you mean you are finding them?' a frustrated Raman Sharma asked. His voice echoed inside the small conference room of his Jalandhar office.

'Sir, both of them are missing from last forty-eight hours. We are trying our best to find them,' Partap replied.

'What the hell is happening? Why are the culprits ahead of us?' Sharma said.

'We just need some more time, sir,' replied Partap.

'Take your time, but the department wants results at the earliest,' Sharma said and concluded the meeting. He updated Saqib Ahmed about the current situation over phone and requested him to demand the file from IG, which Partap had submitted to him. The ADGP cum OSD of the Chief Minister of Punjab immediately called the IG.

'Good evening sir, how are you?' Gupta asked in a made-up polite tone.

'I am fine, Gupta,' Saqib said. 'But I will be even better if you submit the file which Partap had given to you.'

'Which file, sir?' Gupta asked innocently.

'You know it well,' Saqib said.

'Sir, Partap hasn't given me any file,' Gupta refused straightway.

'So, you're implying that Partap is lying?' Saqib said.

'I don't know why, but, yes sir,' Gupta replied.

'I know very well who is lying. You will gain nothing by protecting the culprits Gupta,' Saqib said and hung up the phone. He understood that the IG must have destroyed a very valuable piece of information, which could have acted as primary evidence to put all culprits behind bars. He called Rajan Sharma and informed him what IG Gupta had said.

This was a major setback for the investigating team. Partap, unaffected by the outcome, went to the office of the chairman of the authorisation committee – Prem Prasad Mahajan – to question him about the ingenuine cases found by the range DIGs.

'Here are the details of the ingenuine cases found by the members of the SIT. May I know on what grounds you approved them?' Partap asked, sliding a piece of paper towards the chairman, as the two sat in the principal's office before noon.

'When cases come to us, their documents are already attested by the magistrate. Affidavits are prepared by well-qualified advocates. Taking them into consideration, we approve the cases. It is not our duty to re-verify the credentials which are already verified by the magistrate,' replied Mahajan confidently. 'Every case, which is backed by proper documentation, is genuine for us.'

'So, you never reject cases, right?' Partap asked.

'A number of times we have rejected case files which didn't have proper documents,' replied Mahajan confidently.

Partap knew that the chairman was playing ball, but he didn't have any concrete proof against him at that time. Had he got the evidence file, things would have become easier. Partap tried to grill Mahajan for some more time, but the clever man did not falter at all. A disappointed SP then headed back to his office.

Partap's move to interrogate the chairman of the authorisation committee was criticised by the then health minister K.C. Monga. He openly made a statement before the press that no one could blame the authorisation committee for the fake affidavits submitted before kidney donations. He said that affidavits didn't come under the jurisdiction of the committee. The SIT was surprised by such comments of a minister and how an investigation was affecting him.

The task to unearth the kidney scam was becoming difficult for the SIT as none of the teams could find concrete evidences anywhere. Slowly, it was discovered that not only Sucha and Rajbir, but almost all the donors involved in ingenuine cases who had some time or another complained about their kidney donation had disappeared one by one. This was a huge disappointment for the SIT.

If Saqib had permitted Partap to involve donors in investigation as requested by him earlier, things would have been different. But the department had its boundaries. Manjit Singh and the students, who were closely following every development, were left disappointed. The brutal killing of Baljit Rana in broad daylight, forceful kidney removal of Manjit Singh and attacks on students – the perpetrators of the kidney scam had always been a step ahead. Where the students and Manjit Singh were hopeless, Dr Bhasin and Prem Prasad were delighted by the failure of the SIT's investigation.

Prem Prasad called up Bhasin and told him about the investigation he had faced in his office. The kingpin lauded him for the way he handled everything. Dr Bhasin was keeping a close eye on the working of the SIT through his sources in the police department and instructing his staff accordingly. So far, everything was under control. He was on the brink of defeating the police once again, when Sukhjeet Singh, a team member of the SIT, raided his private clinic.

This was an unexpected move by the police. Though Bhasin had destroyed all the illegal records from his clinic, he was unhappy with this move. Everything was searched thoroughly at his clinic, but nothing was found.

When the team was about to leave, Sukhjeet – who was about to close the patients' records register –opened it quickly once again. He noticed that something was rubbed off in front of the name of one of the patients. When he examined carefully, he saw that in front of a patient named Parkash, a word 'died' was rubbed off and 'discharged and referred to Jhakhar Hospital' was written over it. Sukhjeet became suspicious and immediately rushed to Jhakhar Hospital.

Once at the hospital, he asked the staff to hand over the personal file of Parkash. When he examined the file, he was baffled to see that Parkash was declared dead in it. This was a serious discrepancy in the records. A dead donor was discharged by the hospital on 9 July 2001.

He immediately called Partap and updated him about the development, who then instructed Sukhjeet to arrest all the employees involved in maintaining the hospital records. When the staff members were interrogated, they accepted that the patient had died in the hospital, but at the same time said that word the word 'discharged' was written by mistake. None of them gave any statement which could be used as an evidence in the kidney scam.

Partap went a step ahead and asked Sukhjeet to send a police team to patient's address in UP to confirm whether his family members know about the truth. Within two days, the team informed Partap Singh that they didn't know about his death, as they never got his dead body. All this while, they had been thinking the man had deliberately gone missing owing to domestic problems. This was a major breakthrough for the police. On the basis of this information, Partap ordered further interrogation of the employees of Jhakhar Hospital. Only this time, a tough one.

When Dr Bhasin came to know about the latest development, he was petrified. He had never expected that a small mistake would land him in big trouble. The kingpin knew that his game would be destroyed if any of his staff members spilled beans about his illegal activities. He wanted to stop everything, but it was too late now. One of his staff members finally gave up at the slightest torture by the police and confessed everything.

The tables had turned for the first time!

According to Dr Bhasin's hospital staff member, Parkash had died at the operation table and his body was cremated as 'unclaimed' by one their associates named Nathu. The records of Durgiana Mandir cremation ground further confirmed his confession. The SIT had gathered a major evidence. Everyone in Dr Basin's team was terrified now. The doctors based in other states associated with Dr Bhasin started to call him frantically. They asked him to save them. Dr Bhasin told everyone to stay calm. He still had faith in his political contacts.

His faith was shattered soon when none of his political friends who had benefitted from the trade came forward to help him. They left him out in the open.

A meeting of the SIT was called by Saqib Ahmed where he lauded the efforts of Sukhjeet Singh in procuring the vital evidence. He gave permission to the SIT to interrogate all the doctors of Jhakhar and other suspected hospitals where kidney transplants were done, so that more evidence could be dug out.

'Sir, I think we should arrest Dr Bhasin!' Partap said.

'Not yet. He is a big name. We cannot arrest him with just this piece of evidence. He will just pass the buck onto someone working under him and scot free. If you wish to arrest him, find out more against him!' Saqib said and Partap nodded.

In the coming days, the doctors employed at various hospitals were questioned by the SIT, but none of them revealed anything about illegal kidney transplants. Every time a doctor refused his involvement in the kidney scandal, Partap repented on his decision of handing over the file containing all the evidences to IG Gupta. The SIT did not get any further evidence by interrogating the doctors. The concrete proofs to frame charges against Dr Bhasin and Prem Prasad Mahajan were still missing.

One evening, when Partap was sitting in his office working on the case, his runner came inside and informed him that someone had been insisting to meet him in person. Upon enquiring, Partap came to know that the person was the former PA to IG Gupta.

'Send him inside,' Partap said.

An old man who looked retired, almost in his late fifties, barely able to walk straight due to an oversized protruding belly visible in his grey Safari suit, walked inside Partap's office. The SP politely offered him a seat.

'Good evening, sir. My name is Ramesh Chand,' the old man said, still standing.

'Good evening Ramesh ji. What brings you here?' Partap asked, his eyes glued to the file in front of him.

'My conscience, sir,' Ramesh replied, faintly, politely.

Partap lifted his face to look at the man.

'Sir, I always worked with honesty in the initial years of my service, until greed for money took over me,' Ramesh said and Partap listened carefully. 'I learnt an illegal trick of the trade. I would harass people by deliberately delaying their files. I moved their files only when they paid me. It was easy money. At first, it lures you, but then it becomes a habit. One never spends hard-earned money unnecessarily. But when easy money starts pouring in, aspirations increase and one looks for more. But you know what, god sees everything. Illegal money vanishes at double the rate. God punished me as well. My wife fell terminally ill.'

'But why are you telling me all this?' a curious Partap asked, sensing that there was definitely more to this man's story.

'Just to tell you that I am not the same Ramesh anymore,' he replied and opened his arm-slung bag. Partap narrowed his gaze and saw the man take out a file with a half-burnt cover. His eyes widened at the faint realisation.

'An illegal kidney transplant couldn't save my wife. I think it was god's way of punishing me,' Ramesh said, blinking away the tears in his eyes as he kept the file in front of Partap. When he looked carefully and opened the file, he was baffled to see that it was the same file which Partap had given to the IG.

'IG sir had tried to burn it. I recovered it. This file could have given me a lot of money, but as I said earlier, I am not the old Ramesh anymore. Life has already taught me a lesson. IG sir is an evil man. He let my wife die, and sold the donor's kidney to someone less critical, for more money, without letting me know. He justified his act by stating that my wife was going to die anyway, and was imprudent enough to offer me the share from the kidney's trade. He must pay for his sins as I have paid for mine,' Ramesh said and walked out of Partap's office before Partap could say anything.

Ramesh Chand came as a blessing to the SIT. His personal vengeance with the IG opened the closed doors. Partap immediately informed Saqib Ahmed and Sharma about it. Saqib immediately got orders issued from the Chief Minister to suspend Prem Prasad Mahajan from the post of Principal of city Medical College on the basis of the affidavit submitted by Sucha Singh. As soon as he stepped down, an FIR was registered against him and he was arrested and taken on remand. The fresh FIR again mentioned the names of persons previously arrested by Partap, and soon, most of them, including the advocates involved, were also arrested.

A massive manhunt was launched to nab the absconding offenders. A single file had changed everything. Prem Prasad Mahajan, who had dodged Partap previously, was now left wetting his pants. He was kept with the other culprits inside the cell. Partap's officers tried to make him speak, but he didn't confess anything. When Partap came to know about this, he took the task in his own hands.

'How are you, Mr Mahajan? I have just been informed that you are not cooperating?' Partap said as he stepped inside the cell. Prem Prasad Mahajan refrained from making an eye contact with him.

'Ask all the suspects to remove their clothes,' Partap said to one his officers. Every suspect, except Mahajan, started removing their clothes. How could a former chairman and principal remove his clothes in front of everyone, including some who worked under him? He kept on standing still, as if he hadn't heard anything.

'Mr Mahajan, the order is for everyone,' Partap said strictly and gestured him to remove his clothes. Mahajan understood that he couldn't escape and started to unbutton his shirt. Slowly, he removed it. When it came to removing pants, his hands stopped. He didn't want to get himself humiliated like this. This was when Partap Singh went to him and told him that if he cooperated with the police, he would be spared such humiliation in future.

Prem Prasad Mahajan finally agreed and confessed everything to the police. He confessed that he worked with Dr Bhasin on commission basis and used to get thirty thousand rupees for approving every case. Dr Ranjit Gargi, head of forensic science department and the member of authorisation committee was also involved with him. He also confessed that Dr Bhasin was the chief mastermind and main beneficiary of the kidney scam. He told Partap that the recipients not only belonged to Punjab, but often came from other states and countries as well.

Prem Prasad Mahajan's confession was enough to frame charges against Dr Bhasin and others. The SIT registered an FIR against them. As soon as the infamous kidney surgeon – who was constantly updated by his contacts in the police – got the information of an FIR against him, he decided to flee from the country. He immediately asked his driver to take him out of the city and then towards New Delhi.

On the way to New Delhi, he called his agent to book a ticket of any available flight to London that evening. Dr Bhasin successfully went past the boundary of Punjab and took a sigh of relief. When the police reached his office, they were given no concrete answer by his staff about his whereabouts. When one of the officers thrashed the manager of Jhakhar Hospital, he informed that all he knew was that Dr Bhasin had gone out of the city.

The officer immediately informed Partap about the development, who sent a message across every police station of Punjab to look for Dr Bhasin. Within no time, roadblocks were established throughout Punjab and every vehicle was searched on the borders of Punjab. But it was too late. Dr Pawan Bhasin had fled out of the state already.

Dr Bhasin reached New Delhi after eight hours and headed straight towards the airport. He took a deep breath when he entered the terminal and went for security check. Within the next hour, he boarded the flight to London.

The kingpin had once again fooled the police and fled.

The aircraft was soon speeding up on the runway and took off in no time.

Dr Bhasin was saved! The mastermind of the kidney scam was fleeing the country after successfully carrying out a two-hundred crore kidney scam. Even though it was the end of the road for his established business, he was satisfied that he had made enough money out of the scam already to settle in London and live the rest of his life carefree.

As soon as the flight was mid-air, Bhasin fell asleep. After about thirty minutes into the flight, an announcement was made by the crew that the aircraft was scheduled to land due to some technical emergency. When Bhasin looked out of the window, he could see a familiar landscape below. The airplane was landing in Amritsar. Dr Bhasin was terrified to see this.

The sleep in his eyes vanished in a jiffy. When the aircraft landed, police officials came on board and arrested him.

This time, Manjit and the students had sensed that Dr Bhasin could run away from the country and they had conveyed the same to Partap. Since Partap was already busy, Manjit and the students had taken it upon themselves to carry out round-the-clock surveillance of Dr Bhasin. All this while, when Partap had been busy with the SIT, a fool-proof plan was orchestrated by Manjit which involved sending Bhasin's driver on an emergency leave with the help of a false message of the driver's mother's death. As part of the plan, Rahul – who had grown beard to change his appearance – was employed as Bhasin's driver. Afraid at first and almost on the verge of getting busted, Rahul pulled off his role efficiently as time went by.

On his way to New Delhi, Rahul had already given a call to Partap when they had to stop for fuel on the outskirts of the capital. Rahul, posing as Bhasin's driver, had eavesdropped his conversation with the travel agent and had conveyed the flight details to Partap, who in turn passed on the information to Saqib. The OSD, through the Chief Minister and then Central Aviation Minister had conveyed the message to the Delhi airport.

When he had received the information that Dr Bhasin had boarded a flight to London, he had requested the authorities to re-route it so that the culprit could be caught.

Dr Bhasin was taken on fourteen days remand by the police and Partap had efficiently made him confess everything in the coming days. Police, after obtaining the addresses of the hideouts from him, nabbed all the absconding offenders and recorded their statements. During the raid on one such hideout, a deadly shootout ensued. That left Ricky Bhatia, Tinku and Chandu dead, while Raju was critically injured. Nathu was apprehended from his tea stall.

Dr Bhasin was further charged with causing death of patients. All his associate doctors, including Dr Gargi were either apprehended or they surrendered before the police one by one. A couple of corrupt police officials, including SHO Sanjay Beri, were arrested and expelled from service.

The biggest human organ trade racket of India was finally busted by the police by arresting all the culprits as well as the kingpin.

The Chief Minister of Punjab lauded the efforts of the Special Investigation Team. The ruling party accredited the success to its own efforts and decisions. Manjit Singh, the students and SP Partap Singh finally emerged victorious, against all odds.

Families of many poor donors who had died and had been illegally cremated were informed in the subsequent days. Sucha Singh, Rajbir Singh and rickshaw puller Hardial Singh were never found.

***

Partap Singh received a call on his mobile phone one evening while he was about to leave his office. The caller ID displayed 'private number'.

'Good evening, SP Partap speaking,' Partap answered.

'I was unsure the case file would reach you in time,' a low-pitched voice, unrecognisable to Partap, spoke these words.

'Who is it?' a confused Partap asked.

'A friend of the department,' the man said. 'More importantly, an enemy of Bhasin.'

'Give me your name,' Partap asked loudly. 'Stop playing around!'

'You did a good job, Partap Singh,' the man said. 'It's just sad that some people had to die. But do not worry, compensation has reached Sucha Singh's family and the families of others as well. I appreciate your efforts in fulfilling my dream of destroying Bhasin.'

'What are you—' before Partap could speak, the call got disconnected. The caller could never be traced.

***

References

Several newspapers reported the scam and the findings of the police and SIT. Some of them are reproduced here.

गुर्दा भी गया और पैसे भी नहीं मि

■ राजू का गुर्दा निकाल लिया लेकिन पैसा एक भी नहीं मिला, रवि का सौदा 70 हजार में तय हुआ लेकिन 30 हजार मि

जेल में बंद किडनी डोनर रवि, राजू व राजकुमार। तीनों को शुक्रवार को अदालत में पेशी के लिए लाया गया।

Kidney racket spread beyond Indian border

Vishal Rambani
Amritsar, September 23

THE RECENTLY unearthed kidney racket spread its tentacles beyond the border of the country if the preliminary reports are to be believed. Interrogation of the accused revealed that apart from Indians, Nepalese and Bangladeshi nationals were also members of the racket, which supplied kidneys to even foreign customers. Sources said that two more rackets of this kind were also operating in the city.

Sources said that Bangladeshi and Nepali nationals were also working for Yogesh alias Tinku, the kingpin of the racket. It was easy to find 'cheap donors' in these poor countries and Tinku apparently made a huge profit in such deals, they said. Tinku used the 'langar' of the Golden Temple and other religious places to feed the 'donors', the sources said.

Sources added that the investigations had revealed that foreigners and NRIs from England, Canada and Nepal also obtained kidneys through Tinku, showing false addresses in India. The name of Sri Pandey, a Nepali national who got a kidney by stating a false address in Lucknow also surfaced in the investigation.

Meanwhile, sources said the accused were now running from pillar to post, pulling strings and approaching their political patrons to hush up the case.

It is pertinent to mention that in 2000 Kunwar Vijay Partap Singh – now posted here as SP City I – had busted a kidney racket at Amritsar. However, he was transferred while the investigations were in progress; nearly 18 people had been arrested by then.

SP City-I Kunwar Vijay Partap said the police had got the names of some foreigners in the preliminary investigations; he however refused to divulge details. The SP added that two more gangs were operating in the city and would be nabbed soon. He added that there was no political pressure to hush up the case.

Kidney racket inquiry 'fallout': IGP shifted

HT Correspondent
Chandigarh, December 18

THE PUNJAB government today ordered the transfer of IGP (Border Range) Rajan Gupta after his role in investigations in the Amritsar kidney racket came under a cloud. Gupta will be replaced by IGP (Crime) Chander Shekhar with immediate effect. A decision in this regard was taken at a high-level meeting after the kidney racket was discussed threadbare.

It is learnt that the transfer of IGP Gupta has been effected due to his alleged involvement in shielding the accused in the kidney racket, which was unearthed recently by SP (City), Amritsar, Kunwar Vijay Partap Singh. This has been done to ensure a free and fair investigation in the case, a senior official said.

A high-level meeting called by OSD, Law and Order, A.A. Siddiqui, today discussed various ways to further investigate the scam. A team of three officials, including SP (Detective) Hoshiarpur, DSP, Jalandhar and SP (City), Amritsar, has been constituted under IGP, Zonal, Jalandhar, S.K. Sharma, to complete the inquiry within a stipulated period.

It may be mentioned that the case, which was being investigated by SP (City), Amritsar, had been given to the Crime Branch of the Punjab Police and later transferred to the Vigilance Bureau. However, when the CM returned from Gujarat, he was surprised to know that the case had been transferred to the VB without his approval. Last week, he once again ordered the transfer of the case to the OSD, Law and Order, Siddiqui.

A | The Times of India

669 kidney transplants conducted in Ludhiana

By Harpreet K Kang
Times News Network

Ludhiana: Ever since the authorization committee began functioning from December 12, 1998, 669 cases of kidney transplant had been granted permission.

Of these, 445 permissions were granted to DMC hospital alone, and another 47 to CMC hospital.

The DMC authorities claim that 136 of these cases had donors from their spouse, father, mother, brother, sister, son, and daughter, while 309 were by unrelated donors. At CMC, 24 were related sponsors, and 23 unrelated donors.

Civil surgeon S N Tiwari said that on December 21, 2002, the present authorization committee had received another set of new guidelines from Director, Medical Education and Research (DMER), Chandigarh, which are being incorporated in the permission system. It is learnt that most of procedures suggested to be followed vide new guidelines were largely based on methodology and procedures, which were being followed by the authorization committee.

Police had removed all the documents from DMC hospital on January 16 and took them to IGP S K Sharma at Jalandhar. Meanwhile, principal, DMC hospital, S C Ahuja said that the Human Organ Transplant Authorization Committee based in Ludhiana, constituted by the state government, consists of four members. It had been granting permission as per the guidelines issued in this regard from time to time, he added.

He further said that if any difficulty was felt then the committee used to refer the matter to the DRME for seeking clarification and guidance.

infamous kidney scam and recorded his statement before Judicial Magistrate (Class I) Ranjit Kaur under Section 164 of the CrPC.

IMA Secretary Dr Rakesh Madan told *Hindustan Times* that the medical fraternity understood that Dr Arora had taken this step to save his own skin. Dr Arora, who was member of Authorisation Committee by virtue of his post, retired a few months back.

Meanwhile, on the call given by IMA and other medical and paramedical staff associations, the health services remained crippled throughout the district in all government and private hospitals in protest against the arrest of Government Medical College Principal and Authorisation Committee head Dr O P Mahajan and leading kidney surgeon P.K. Sarin even as a sessions court today stayed arrests of six doctors, including Civil Surgeon K.K. Sharma, who had applied for anticipatory bail, till January 22.

On the other hand, police today involved the clerical staff of local Kakkar Hospital in the investigation related to the kidney scam case. Sources disclosed that the clerical staff was taken to the police station to get their ... was rounded up for questioning and allowed to go after a short while. Police have already taken away data available on computers in the hospital.

It may be mentioned that Dr Sarin worked in Kakkar Hospital and a majority of the kidney transplant cases have taken place in this hospital since the enactment of Transplantation of Human Organs Act, 1994. Following the arrest of Dr Sarin, *continued on page 3*

Poor donors were cheated of fees

...RAM JIT SINGH &
...TINDER KAUR TUR
...ANDIGARH/AMRITSAR, JANUARY 19

IF VIP kidney patients came from as far as Nepal, Orissa, Maharashtra to seek salvation in Amritsar's infamous Kakkar Hospital, the poor labourers, ...o sold their kidneys for a song, ...re sourced from as far as Delhi's ...andni Chowk, kept in virtual captivity in a pear orchard before being ...rved up on the operation table.

Investigations by *The Indian Express* reveal that advocate Rajan Puri used to lure labourers from the labour chowk at Chandi Chowk by offering them Rs 200 per day. Once they got to the pear orchard situated on the Jalandhar-Amritsar bypass, they were given Rs 100 per day and then offered a sum of Rs 40,000-Rs 1 lakh to "donate their kidney".

"It is a clear case of cheating as the labourers were never given the full amount promised by the brokers," said R.S. Bains, an advocate with the Punjab and Haryana High Court and a member of the investigations conducted by the Punjab Human Rights Organisation (PHRO).

CONTINUED ON PAGE 5

SIT seizes 103 certificates from Sareen clinic

THE Special Investigation Team probing the kidney racket today seized 103 blank certificates during the raid of Dr P.K. Sareen's private clinic, here. The SIT spokesperson said these blank certificates were signed by Dr Sareen and Dr Jain. "These certificates stated that no monetary transactions had taken place in the kidney transplant. But strangely, these did not contain the names of the donors or the recipients." He added: "This shows the premeditated nature of the transplant where the certificates were kept ready for the illegal operation, and the complicity of the doctors."

Meanwhile, the SIT has issued arrest warrants against Dr Brushan Aggarwal, who worked under Dr Sareen and is suspected to be involved in the racket. "Right from the stage of establishing contact with the middlemen to making payments, Dr Aggarwal was involved," the spokesperson added. The SIT has given orders for the search of Dr Aggarwal's house. Soon, it will also initiate proceedings to declare the accused doctors who are avoiding arrest proclaimed offenders.

Poor donors were cheated of fees

Donors spoken to by this newspaper revealed that threats to kill were given to them in case they tried to back out of the kidney transplant. "A case of Bagicha Singh, a young boy of 17 has also come to light in June 2000, who was kidnapped by middlemen and later operated upon at the New Ruby Hospital by a team of Dr Arjinder Singh and Dr H.S. Butalia. However, in the age of Bagicha Singh was shown as 22 years in the affidavit submitted to the Authorisation Committee," said Serbjeet Singh, principal investigator for the PHRO.

After the operation, the poor donors were discharged and kept in the 27 safehouses. "They were attended to here by junior doctors. Sample medicines, which have only 20 per cent strength, were administered leading to various complications and even deaths," said Serbjeet.

What has also come to light is that in case a Muslim patient was in need of a kidney, the donor's name was changed to suit the religious sensibilities. According to the PHRO, nine FIRs have been filed in the kidney scam but not even in one of the cases has the police arrested a recipient although many of the poor donors have been bundled into jail. "The FIR lodged in June 2000 in the kidney case gave a scare to the kidney doctors. They then made it a point to ask their well-heeled VIPs to procure a reccommendation letter from MPs/MLAs and the like stating that they personally knew the donor/recipient. This strategy was meant to ensure that in case of trouble, the involvement of these VIPs giving recommendation letters would hush up case," said Serbjeet.

Migrant labour that came into Amritsar used to get in touch with the labour union leaders at the community centres. "It used to begin with blood donation. Union leaders in touch with the kidney scam brokers would then cajole these labourers into donating their kidney by offering big sums. The blood group of the labourer was matched with that of the patient and the broker was paid between Rs 50,0000-Rs 1 lakh," said Serbjeet.

PHRO investigations showed that certain hospitals all over India referred kidney patients to Amritsar on the promise that a transplant would cost just Rs 5 lakh there against Rs 10 lakh in New Delhi where the regulations were stricter. "Compared to the 1,922 transplant cases in Amritsar, only 650 cases were recorded in nine hospitals in Delhi in the same period," said Serbjeet.

ਮਨੁੱਖੀ ਅੰਗਾਂ ਦੇ ਸਕੈਂਡਲ 'ਚ ਸ਼ਤਰੂਘਨ ਸਿਨਹਾ ਨੂੰ ਪੰਜਾਬ ਸਰਕਾਰ 'ਤੇ ਸ਼ੱਕ

ਨਵੀਂ ਦਿੱਲੀ, 5 ਸਤੰਬਰ (ਯੂ.ਐੱਨ.ਆਈ.)— ਕੇਂਦਰੀ ਸਿਹਤ ਮੰਤਰੀ ਸ਼ਤਰੂਘਨ ਸਿਨਹਾ ਨੇ ਅੱਜ ਕਿਹਾ ਕਿ ਮਨੁੱਖੀ ਅੰਗਾਂ ਦੀ ਵਿਕਰੀ ਦੇ ਇੰਗਲੈਂਡ ਨਾਲ ਸੰਬੰਧਤ ਸਕੈਂਡਲ 'ਚ ਉਨ੍ਹਾਂ ਨੂੰ ਪੰਜਾਬ ਪ੍ਰਸ਼ਾਸਨ ਦੀ ਸ਼ਮੂਲੀਅਤ ਦਾ ਸ਼ੱਕ ਹੈ। ਉਨ੍ਹਾਂ ਯੂ.ਐੱਨ.ਆਈ. ਨਾਲ ਗੱਲਬਾਤ 'ਚ ਕਿਹਾ, "ਹੈਰਾਨੀ ਦੀ ਗੱਲ ਹੈ ਕਿ ਪੰਜਾਬ ਸਰਕਾਰ ਨੇ ਇਸ ਸਕੈਂਡਲ ਬਾਰੇ ਹੁਣ ਤਕ ਕੁਝ ਨਹੀਂ ਕਿਹਾ ਪਰ ਮੈਨੂੰ ਅਫਸੋਸ ਨਾਲ ਕਹਿਣਾ ਪੈਂਦਾ ਹੈ ਕਿ ਅਜਿਹੀਆਂ ਘਟਨਾਵਾਂ ਪ੍ਰਸ਼ਾਸਨ ਦੀ ਮਿਲੀਭੁਗਤ ਤੋਂ ਬਿਨਾ ਨਹੀਂ ਹੋ ਸਕਦੀਆਂ।"

ਪਿਛਲੇ ਸ਼ੁੱਕਰਵਾਰ ਭਾਰਤੀ ਮੂਲ ਦੇ ਇਕ ਰਿਟਾਇਰਡ ਡਾਕਟਰ ਭਗਤ ਸਿੰਘ ਮੱਕੜ ਨੂੰ ਬਰਤਾਨੀਆ ਦੀ ਜਨਰਲ ਮੈਡੀਕਲ ਕੌਂਸਲ (ਜੀ.ਐੱਮ.ਸੀ.) ਨੇ ਮਨੁੱਖੀ ਅੰਗਾਂ ਦੀ ਵਿਕਰੀ ਵਿਚ ਦੋਸ਼ੀ ਪਾਇਆ ਸੀ। ਉਸ ਨੇ ਖੁਫੀਆ ਪੱਤਰਕਾਰਾਂ ਨੂੰ ਕਥਿਤ ਤੌਰ 'ਤੇ ਇਹ ਦੱਸਿਆ ਸੀ ਕਿ ਉਹ ਵਿਦੇਸ਼ 'ਚੋਂ ਜੀਊਂਦੇ ਬੰਦੇ ਦੀ ਕਿਡਨੀ ਖ਼ਰੀਦ ਸਕਦਾ ਹੈ।

ਇਕ ਹੋਰ ਡਾਕਟਰ ਜਰਨੈਲ ਸਿੰਘ ਨੇ ਵੀ ਇਸੇ ਮਹੀਨੇ ਜੀ.ਐੱਮ.ਸੀ. ਅੱਗੇ ਪੇਸ਼ ਹੋਣਾ ਹੈ। ਉਸ 'ਤੇ ਦੋਸ਼ ਹੈ ਕਿ ਉਸ ਵਲੋਂ ਮਾਰਚ 'ਚ ਜਲੰਧਰ ਤੋਂ ਪ੍ਰਾਪਤ ਕਿਡਨੀ 69 ਸਾਲਾ ਬ੍ਰਿਟਿਸ਼ ਨਾਗਰਿਕ ਦਰਸ਼ਨ ਸਿੰਘ ਸੰਧੂ ਨੂੰ ਫਿਟ ਕਰਨ ਸਮੇਂ ਉਸ ਦੀ ਮੌਤ ਹੋ ਗਈ। ਖ਼ਬਰਾਂ ਮੁਤਾਬਕ ਅਮਰਜੀਤ ਸਿੰਘ ਨੇ ਇਹ ਕਿਡਨੀ ਸੰਧੂ ਵਲੋਂ ਉਸ ਨੂੰ ਬਰਤਾਨੀਆ 'ਚ ਨੌਕਰੀ ਦਿਵਾਉਣ ਦਾ ਲਾਲਚ ਦੇਣ 'ਤੇ ਦਾਨ ਕੀਤੀ ਸੀ।

(ਬਾਕੀ ਸਫ਼ਾ 10 ਕਾਲਮ 4 'ਤੇ)

ਮਨੁੱਖੀ ਅੰਗਾਂ ਦੇ...

ਸ੍ਰੀ ਸਿਨਹਾ ਨੇ ਅਜਿਹੇ ਦੋਸ਼ਾਂ 'ਚ ਸੂਬਾ ਸਰਕਾਰ ਦੀ ਵਿਲਮਠ ਨੂੰ ਵੀ ਰੱਦ ਨਹੀਂ ਕੀਤਾ। ਉਨ੍ਹਾਂ ਕਿਹਾ ਕਿ ਮਨੁੱਖੀ ਅੰਗ ਦੀ ਵਿਕਰੀ ਦੇ ਧੰਦੇ ਦੀ ਕਾਮਯਾਬੀ ਇਸੇ ਕਰ ਕੇ ਹੋ ਸਕਦੀ ਹੈ। ਉਨ੍ਹਾਂ ਅੱਗੇ ਕਿਹਾ ਕਿ ਮਨੁੱਖੀ ਅੰਗ ਦੀ ਕਿਸੇ ਬੇਨਤੀ ਨੂੰ ਸਖ਼ਤੀ ਨਾਲ ਵਾਚਣ ਤੇ ਪਰਖਣ ਦੀ ਲੋੜ ਹੈ।

ਸ੍ਰੀ ਸਿਨਹਾ ਨੇ ਕਿਹਾ ਕਿ ਨਵੀਂ ਦਿੱਲੀ ਦੇ 9 ਅਧਿਕਾਰਤ ਹਸਪਤਾਲਾਂ 'ਚ ਅਪ੍ਰੈਲ, 2000 ਤੋਂ ਸਾਢੇ ਛੇ ਸੌ ਅੰਗ ਬਦਲੇ ਗਏ ਹਨ ਪਰ ਕਿਸੇ ਕੇਸ 'ਚ ਅਜਿਹੀ ਬੇਕਾਇਦਗੀ ਦੀ ਸ਼ਿਕਾਇਤ ਨਹੀਂ ਮਿਲੀ।

ਤਾਂ ਵੀ, ਉਨ੍ਹਾਂ ਮਨੁੱਖੀ ਅੰਗ ਬਦਲਣ ਦੇ 1994 ਦੇ ਕਾਨੂੰਨ 'ਚ ਸੋਧ ਕਰਨ ਦੀ ਗੱਲ ਨਹੀਂ ਕਹੀ। ਉਨ੍ਹਾਂ ਕਿਹਾ ਕਿ ਇਸ 'ਤੇ ਪਾਬੰਦੀ ਨਾਲ ਉਨ੍ਹਾਂ ਲੋਕਾਂ ਦਾ ਨੁਕਸਾਨ ਹੋਵੇਗਾ ਜਿਨ੍ਹਾਂ ਨੂੰ ਸੱਚਮੁਚ ਬਦਲਵੇਂ ਅੰਗ ਦਰਕਾਰ ਹਨ।

NRI flights landed in Amritsar

By Ajay Bharadwaj
TIMES NEWS NETWORK

KIDNEY SCAM

Chandigarh: The investigation into the clandestine kidney-sale in Punjab took a new turn when officials found out that the kidney recipients included atleast 50 NRIs, who came from as far off as Canada and European countries.

The special investigation team (SIT) is looking into two chartered flights, which supposedly came to Amritsar last year, carrying 20-25 NRIs, who received kidneys here.

The SIT is browsing through the records seized from the Kakkar hospital to ascertain the information. "The task is slightly arduous as the NRI recipients might have been operated upon on fake names, given the kind of situation at that time", said a senior officer.

As the Amritsar-based authorisation committee is not allowed to clear cases of kidney transplants of people living outside Amritsar, Jalandhar and Gurdaspur districts, the SIT has not ruled out the possibility of the NRIs being wrongly shown as Amritsar residents, the practice which the middlemen carried out for kidney recipients from outside the state.

Preliminary information has indicated that a flight came from Canada and another from France.

Inspector general of police (Jalandhar range) S K Sharma, who is supervising the investigation, confirmed that the SIT was working on the information, but refused to comment further on the matter.

Meanwhile, the SIT has identified the Amritsar-based lawyer, George Switt, who used to forge magistrate's signatures on fake affidavits produced by donors. He was working in tandem with another advocate, Rajan Puri, in preparing fake affidavits, which were submitted before the authorisation committee on behalf of both kidney donors and recipients.

The committee is already in the dock for accepting fake affidavits without questioning their validity and contents at any stage.

The SIT is still hunting for five accused including three doctors, P K Jain, Bhushan Agarwal and Bhupinder Singh. All of them have been absconding after the stay on their arrests was vacated by court last week.

Monday, September 23, 2002

PUNJAB

Kidney racket busted in Amritsar; 14 held

HT Correspondent
Amritsar, September 22

WITH THE arrest of 14 persons involved in the sale of kidneys, the Amritsar police claim to have unearthed a scam which could involve some reputed doctors in the city. The scam has also raised questions about the role of the Health Department committee that screens organ donations.

Among those arrested are three agents and three former donors now employed by the agents. The others were prospective donors who had come for a deal.

SP City-I Kunwar Vijay Partap said the police, who were acting on a tip-off, raided Gol Bagh and Friends Colony. Gang leader Yogesh alias Tinku of Karnal succeeded in fleeing, but was subsequently nabbed in a special operation, he said. Police have registered a case under Section 420 and 120-B and 18, 19, 20 of Transplantation of Human Organs Act.

S.K. SHARMA/HT

Former kidney donors, now part of the racket, show surgery marks.

Talking to *Hindustan Times*, Raju Mehra of Ujjain admitted that he had sold one of his kidneys in Amritsar about 4 years back and had been selling blood for the last two years. Mehra said that he had sold his kidney to local resident Roshan Lal through a middleman named Chandan. The deal was fixed at Rs 40,000 and he was operated upon at Kakkar Hospital, he said, adding that the kidney was subsequently transplanted in Roshan Lal's 24-year-old daughter Archana.

Ravi Kumar Yadav (25) of Dehradun was initially disqualified by the donor screening committee after he revealed his original name during the interview. However, the agent later settled the matter with the committee and he was operated at New Ruby Hospital in Jalandhar, he said. To convince the committee his name was shown as Mohammed Salim, a long-time servant of Delhi resident Mohammed Takali who was supposed to receive the organ. Yadav too received Rs 40,000 from the agent, though he believes the original amount was much higher.

However, Rampur resident Raju was cheated both by the agent and the customer. Though the deal was finalised at Rs 40,000, he got only Rs 15,000 as the customer left Amritsar while he was still recovering in hospital. Raju, who said he was given VIP treatment till the operation at Kakkar Hospital, said Laxman, a crony of Tinku, had mediated the deal with C.B. Pandey of Lucknow. Though he was assured the remaining Rs 25,000 would be paid in a few weeks, they never were.

The SP said investigation had proved that the arrested donors had given false affidavits about their identity. They had also testified that no money had changed hands, he added. Screening committee chairman and Principal of the Government Medical College O.P. Mahajan said there was nothing wrong in the screening process. The panel signed documents only after getting the donor's affidavit attested by a Magistrate, he said.

The SP said gang leader Tinku had mediated in over 300 kidney sales. Tinku was residing in a rented house in Friends Colony and hired many donors as middlemen. It is these middlemen who bring in 'donors' from all over India, the SP said. The prospective donors who have been arrested have been identified as Amit Kumar of Muzzafarabad, Raj Kumar, Dilip Singh and Upinder from Bihar, Gaurav from Haryana, Ravi Sahni from UP, Umesh from Nagpur and Prem Kumar from Manipur.

Meanwhile, Kakkar Hospital management said their name had cropped up since it was the only hospital that had been granted permission for kidney transplant in the city.

ਗੁਰਦੇ ਵੇਚਣ ਵਾਲੇ ਗਿਰੋਹ ਦੇ ਸਰਗਣੇ ਸਣੇ 14 ਗ੍ਰਿਫ਼ਤਾਰ

ਅੰਮ੍ਰਿਤਸਰ, 22 ਸਤੰਬਰ (ਕੁਮਿਤਾ)— ਐਸ ਪੀ. ਸਿਟੀ-1 ਕੁੰਵਰ ਵਿਜੇ ਪ੍ਰਤਾਪ ਸਿੰਘ ਨੇ ਆਪਣੀ ਪੁਲਸ ਪਾਰਟੀ ਸਮੇਤ ਮੁਖਬਰ ਖਾਸ ਦੀ ਇਤਲਾਹ 'ਤੇ ਜਗ੍ਹਾ-ਜਗ੍ਹਾ ਛਾਪੇ ਮਾਰ ਕੇ ਕਿਡਨੀ (ਗੁਰਦਾ) ਵੇਚਣ ਵਾਲੇ ਗਿਰੋਹ ਦੇ ਮੁੱਖ ਤਿੰਨ ਵਿਅਕਤੀ ਅਤੇ ਹੋਰ 11 ਵਿਅਕਤੀਆਂ ਨੂੰ ਗ੍ਰਿਫ਼ਤਾਰ ਕਰਨ ਵਿਚ ਭਾਰੀ ਸਫਲਤਾ ਪ੍ਰਾਪਤ ਕੀਤੀ। ਐਸ. ਪੀ. ਸਿਟੀ-1 ਨੇ ਦੱਸਿਆ ਕਿ ਪਿਛਲੇ 6 ਸਾਲਾਂ ਤੋਂ ਕਿਡਨੀ ਵੇਚਣ ਦਾ ਧੰਦਾ ਬੜੇ ਜ਼ੋਰਾਂ ਨਾਲ ਚਲ ਰਿਹਾ ਸੀ ਅਤੇ ਅੱਜ ਤੋਂ ਦੋ ਸਾਲ ਪਹਿਲਾਂ ਵੀ ਉਨ੍ਹਾਂ ਨੇ ਥਾਣਾ ਬੀ ਡਵੀਜ਼ਨ ਵਿਚ ਇਸ ਧੰਦੇ ਵਿਚ ਸ਼ਾਮਲ 18 ਵਿਅਕਤੀਆਂ ਦੇ ਵਿਰੁੱਧ ਕੇਸ ਦਰਜ ਕੀਤਾ। ਇਸ ਵਾਰੀ ਉਨ੍ਹਾਂ ਨੇ ਬੜੇ ਸੋਚ ਵਿਚਾਰ ਨਾਲ ਇਸ ਗੈਂਗ ਦੇ ਸਰਗਣਾ ਟਿੰਕੂ ਵਾਸੀ ਹਰਿਆਣਾ ਜੋ ਕਿ ਹਾਲ ਫਰੈਂਡਜ਼ ਕਾਲੋਨੀ, ਅੰਮ੍ਰਿਤਸਰ, ਲਛਮਣ ਵਾਸੀ ਯੂ. ਪੀ. ਅਤੇ ਰਾਜਕੁਮਾਰ ਵਾਸੀ ਮਥੁਰਾ ਨੂੰ ਮੁਖਬਰ ਖਾਸ ਦੀ ਇਤਲਾਹ 'ਤੇ ਫੜ ਕੇ ਅਤੇ ਉਨ੍ਹਾਂ ਕੋਲੋਂ ਪੁੱਛਗਿੱਛ ਦੌਰਾਨ ਰਾਜੂ ਮਹਿਰਾ ਵਾਸੀ ਉਜੈਨ, ਜਿਸ ਨੇ 40 ਹਜ਼ਾਰ ਰੁਪਏ ਵਿਚ ਅੱਜ ਤੋਂ ਚਾਰ ਸਾਲ ਪਹਿਲਾਂ ਰੌਸ਼ਨ ਲਾਲ ਵਾਸੀ ਅੰਮ੍ਰਿਤਸਰ ਦੀ ਬੇਟੀ ਅਰਚਨਾ ਨੂੰ ਕਿਡਨੀ ਦਿੱਤੀ ਸੀ, ਜਿਸ ਨੂੰ ਅੰਮ੍ਰਿਤਸਰ ਦੇ ਇਕ ਹਸਪਤਾਲ ਵਿਚ ਬਦਲਿਆ ਗਿਆ ਸੀ। ਇਸ ਤਰ੍ਹਾਂ ਰਵੀ ਕੁਮਾਰ ਯਾਦਵ ਵਾਸੀ ਦੇਹਰਾਦੂਨ ਨੇ ਆਪਣੀ ਕਿਡਨੀ 40 ਹਜ਼ਾਰ ਰੁਪਏ ਵਿਚ ਨਿਊ ਰੂਬੀ ਹਸਪਤਾਲ ਜਲੰਧਰ ਵਿਚ ਇਕ ਮਰੀਜ਼ ਮੁਹੰਮਦ ਤਸਕੀਨ ਦਿੱਲੀ ਨੂੰ ਦੇ ਦਿੱਤੀ ਸੀ ਅਤੇ ਗੁਰੂ ਵਾਸੀ ਯੂ. ਪੀ. ਨੇ ਇਕ ਕਿਡਨੀ ਨੇਪਾਲ ਦੇ ਰਹਿਣ ਵਾਲੇ ਇਕ ਮਰੀਜ਼ ਸੀ. ਬੀ. ਪਾਂਡੇ ਨੂੰ 15 ਹਜ਼ਾਰ ਰੁਪਏ ਵਿਚ ਦਿੱਤੀ ਸੀ ਜਿਸ ਨੂੰ ਅੰਮ੍ਰਿਤਸਰ ਦੇ ਕੱਕੜ ਹਸਪਤਾਲ ਵਿਚ ਬਦਲਿਆ ਗਿਆ ਸੀ। ਇਸ ਦੇ ਇਲਾਵਾ ਗੌਰਵ ਵਾਸੀ ਹਰਿਆਣਾ, ਰਵੀ ਵਾਸੀ ਯੂ. ਪੀ., ਉਮੇਸ਼ ਵਾਸੀ ਨਾਗਪੁਰ, ਪ੍ਰੇਮ ਕੁਮਾਰ ਵਾਸੀ ਮਨੀਪੁਰ, ਦਲੀਪ ਵਾਸੀ (ਬਾਕੀ ਸਫ਼ਾ 10 ਕਾਲਮ 2 'ਤੇ)

ਅੰਮ੍ਰਿਤਸਰ 'ਚ ਗੁਰਦੇ ਵੇਚਣ ਦਾ ਧੰਦਾ ਕਰਨ ਵਾਲਿਆਂ ਬਾਰੇ ਜਾਣਕਾਰੀ ਦਿੰਦੇ ਹੋਏ ਐਸ. ਪੀ. ਸਿਟੀ-1 ਕੁੰਵਰ ਵਿਜੇ ਪ੍ਰਤਾਪ ਸਿੰਘ ਅਤੇ (ਸੱਜੇ) ਕਾਬੂ ਕੀਤੇ ਵਿਅਕਤੀਆਂ ਨਾਲ ਪੁਲਸ ਪਾਰਟੀ। (ਫੋਟੋ : ਅਬਦੇਸ਼, ਵਿਕਰਾਂਤ)

ਗੁਰਦੇ ਵੇਚਣ ਵਾਲੇ ਗਿਰੋਹ...

ਕੈਂਸਪੁਰ ਆਦਿ ਦੇ ਇਲਾਵਾ ਅਤੇ ਹੋਰ ਤਿੰਨ ਅਜਿਹੇ ਵਿਅਕਤੀਆਂ ਨੂੰ ਫੜਿਆ ਜੋ ਕਿਡਨੀ ਦੇਣ ਲਈ ਇੰਕੂ ਦੇ ਨਿਰਦੇਸ਼ਾਂ ਦਾ ਇੰਤਜ਼ਾਰ ਕਰ ਰਹੇ ਸੀ।

ਕਿਡਨੀ ਦੇਣ ਵਾਲੇ ਉਪਰੋਕਤ ਤਿੰਨਾਂ ਨੌਜਵਾਨਾਂ ਨੇ ਦੱਸਿਆ ਕਿ ਜਦ ਕਿਡਨੀ ਦੇਣ ਲਈ ਹਸਪਤਾਲ ਵਿਚ ਜਾਂਦੇ ਤਾਂ ਹਸਪਤਾਲ ਦੀ ਕਮੇਟੀ ਦੇ ਸਾਹਮਣੇ ਉਨ੍ਹਾਂ ਦੇ ਦਸਤਖਤ ਕਰਵਾ ਲਏ ਜਾਂਦੇ ਸੀ ਅਤੇ ਕਿਹਾ ਗਿਆ ਸੀ ਕਿ ਅਸੀਂ ਪਿਛਲੇ ਕਈ ਸਾਲਾਂ ਤੋਂ ਇਨ੍ਹਾਂ ਦੇ ਘਰੇਲੂ ਨੌਕਰ ਹਾਂ। ਰਾਜੂ ਵਾਸੀ ਯੂ. ਪੀ. ਨੇ ਦੱਸਿਆ ਕਿ ਜਦੋਂ ਉਹ ਅੰਮ੍ਰਿਤਸਰ ਦੇ ਹਸਪਤਾਲ ਵਿਚ ਕਿਡਨੀ ਦੇਣ ਲਈ ਗਿਆ ਤਾਂ ਉਸ ਨੇ ਸਾਫ਼ ਹੀ ਕਹਿ ਦਿੱਤਾ ਸੀ ਕਿ ਮਰੀਜ਼ ਦੇ ਨਾਲ ਉਸ ਦਾ ਕੋਈ ਲੈਣ-ਦੇਣ ਨਹੀਂ ਹੈ ਉਹ ਕੇਵਲ ਪੈਸਿਆਂ ਲਈ ਹੀ ਕਿਡਨੀ ਵੇਚਣ ਆਇਆ ਹੈ ਪ੍ਰੰਤੂ ਉਸ ਸਮੇਂ ਕਮੇਟੀ ਨੇ ਉਸ ਨੂੰ ਉਥੋਂ ਭਜਾ ਦਿੱਤਾ ਸੀ ਪਰ ਕੁਝ ਦਿਨ ਬਾਅਦ ਹੀ ਦਲਾਲਾਂ ਦੇ ਨਾਲ ਮਿਲੀਭੁਗਤ ਨਾਲ ਉਸ ਦੀ ਕਿਡਨੀ ਦੁਬਾਰਾ 15 ਹਜ਼ਾਰ ਰੁਪਏ ਵਿਚ ਲੈ ਲਈ।

ਇਸ ਤਰ੍ਹਾਂ ਰਾਜੂ ਮਹਿਰਾ ਨੇ ਦੱਸਿਆ ਕਿ ਅੱਜ ਤੋਂ ਚਾਰ ਸਾਲ ਪਹਿਲਾਂ ਉਹ ਆਪਣੀ ਕਿਡਨੀ ਦੇ ਚੁੱਕਿਆ ਸੀ ਅਤੇ ਕਾਫੀ ਦੇਰ ਤੋਂ ਅੰਮ੍ਰਿਤਸਰ ਵਿਚ ਆਇਆ ਹੋਇਆ ਸੀ ਅਤੇ ਮਹਾਰਾਜਾ ਬੈਂਡ ਵਾਲਿਆਂ ਕੋਲ ਨੌਕਰੀ ਕਰਦਾ ਸੀ ਅਤੇ ਆਪਣੇ ਸਰੀਰ ਵਿਚੋਂ ਖ਼ੂਨ ਕੱਢ ਕੇ 230 ਰੁਪਏ ਹਰੇਕ ਬੋਤਲ ਦੇ ਹਿਸਾਬ ਨਾਲ ਰਾਮ ਪ੍ਰਸਾਦ ਨਾਂ ਦੇ ਦਲਾਲ ਨੂੰ ਦਿੰਦਾ ਸੀ। ਉਸ ਨੇ ਕਿਹਾ ਕਿ ਉਹ ਮਹੀਨੇ ਵਿਚ ਚਾਰ ਜਾਂ ਪੰਜ ਵਾਰੀ ਖ਼ੂਨ ਦਿੰਦਾ ਸੀ ਅਤੇ ਦਵਾਈਆਂ ਖਾ ਕੇ ਫਿਰ ਖ਼ੂਨ ਬਣ ਜਾਂਦਾ ਸੀ। ਰਾਮ ਪ੍ਰਸਾਦ ਨਾਂ ਦਾ ਦਲਾਲ ਕੰਪਨੀ ਬਾਗ ਦੇ ਅੰਦਰ ਹੀ ਡ੍ਰਿਪ ਲਗਾ ਕੇ ਉਸ ਦਾ ਖ਼ੂਨ ਕੱਢ ਲੈਂਦਾ ਸੀ। ਉਹ ਕਰੀਬ 200 ਬੋਤਲ ਖ਼ੂਨ ਦੀ ਦੇ ਚੁੱਕਿਆ ਹੈ। ਐਸ. ਪੀ. ਸਿਟੀ-1 ਨੇ ਦੱਸਿਆ ਕਿ ਅੰਮ੍ਰਿਤਸਰ ਵਿਚ ਉਨ੍ਹਾਂ ਦੀ ਇਤਲਾਹ ਮੁਤਾਬਕ ਇਸ ਸਮੇਂ ਤਿੰਨ ਗਿਰੋਹ ਹਨ। ਉਨ੍ਹਾਂ ਵਿਚੋਂ ਇਕ ਗਿਰੋਹ ਦਾ ਅਸੀਂ ਪਰਦਾਫਾਸ਼ ਕਰ ਦਿੱਤਾ ਅਤੇ ਜਲਦੀ ਹੀ ਬਾਕੀ ਦੇ ਦੋ ਗਿਰੋਹਾਂ ਦਾ ਪਰਦਾਫਾਸ਼ ਵੀ ਕਰ ਦਿੱਤਾ ਜਾਵੇਗਾ ਅਤੇ ਉਨ੍ਹਾਂ ਕਿਹਾ ਕਿ ਇਸ ਗਿਰੋਹ ਦੇ ਨਾਲ ਜਿਸ ਕਿਸੇ ਵੀ ਡਾਕਟਰ ਜਾਂ ਹੋਰ ਦਲਾਲ ਜਾਂ ਕਿਸੇ ਹਸਪਤਾਲ ਦਾ ਸੰਬੰਧ ਹੋਵੇਗਾ, ਉਸ ਦੇ ਵਿਰੁੱਧ ਜਲਦ ਤੋਂ ਜਲਦ ਕਾਨੂੰਨੀ ਕਾਰਵਾਈ ਕੀਤੀ ਜਾਵੇਗੀ।

KIDNEY RACKET

Lawyers under scanner for preparing fake affidavits

Vishal Rambani
Amritsar, November 3

AFTER DONORS, recipients and middlemen, it now seems lawyers too were involved in preparing fake affidavits to facilitate the illegal sale of kidneys in this part of the state.

Sources told Hindustan Times that police have found that none of the affidavits that the 'donors' and recipients presented before the Authorisation Committee for the organ transplant were duly attested by the Executive Magistrate.

Sources said the committee had approved more than 700 cases for transplantation in the last two years, including nearly 400 cases this year. Out of these 700 cases, not a single affidavit was registered in the record of the Magistrate Office and in all cases the 'donor' was shown to be a servant of the 'recipient', they added.

SP City-1 Kunwar Vijay Partap confirmed that the affidavits were 'not' registered at the office of the Executive Magistrate and said police would soon arrest the advocates who prepared false affidavits.

Apart from Rajan Puri, who was arrested for making false affidavits, the police have identified at least a dozen more advocates who used to prepare false affidavits; one of them a legal advisor of the hospital where many of the operations were done. Sources said at least four lawyers had made more than 100 false affidavits.

It is learnt that the lawyers used to charge anywhere between Rs 5,000 to 50,000 for preparing a false affidavit. The donors' identities and addresses had been changed to show that they were working with the recipients for the past eight to ten years. In some cases the advocates even changed the religion of the 'donor', like in the case of teenaged Bagicha Singh, who was presented as Raju (20) before the Authorisation Committee after trimming his hair.

OP Mahajan suspended

18-1-03

By Surinder Awasthi
TIMES NEWS NETWORK

KIDNEY SCAM

Chandigarh: The police has sought permission to prosecute arrested Amritsar Medical College principal, OP Mahajan, who had been put under suspension on January 15.

Meanwhile, the Punjab government has indicated that it would scan the role of other members on the authorisation committee, headed by Mahajan, and also of the previous authorisation committees since 1997, when the Act on human organ transplant came into operation in Punjab.

Financial commissioner, medical education and research, Rajesh Chhabra, told Times News Network that he would soon urge inspector general of police SK Sharma to probe the complicity, if any, of the other members of the authorisation committee. He said the police had till now focussed on the nexus between the chairman of the authorisation committee and the network of touts and doctors involved in the kidney scam.

Chhabra said all cases are cleared by majority in the committee but it can't be deduced that all signatories to clearance of transplant cases are party to covert deals. But their role needs to be scanned, he added.

Mahajan had been principal of government medical college for a year and half and, earlier, his two predecessors had headed the committee. One member, who heads the forensic department, had been on all the panels.

Rajkumar Yadav, allegedly a kidney donor who was arrested in October, talking to the media on Friday.

'We were threatened, jailed'

TIMES NEWS NETWORK

Amritsar: "I do not know anything about kidney. Police picked few of us from the railway station. We were threatened and lodged in jail."

Stating this on Friday, Rajkumar Yadav, who was arrested in October last year as a probable donor in the kidney trade scam, alleged that there was no law in Punjab.

Rajkumar, who was produced before the court along with others here, alleged that he along with three more persons had disembarked from the train on October 19, 2002, from where police picked them up. "We were sent to jail where police officials instructed us to state that we had been arrested from Goal Bagh, otherwise they threatened torture."

Another donor Raju, however, said that he was promised Rs 40, 000 but was not paid anything.

● Related reports on page 3

Spare donors: CM

Chandigarh: Taking a humanistic view, chief minister Amarinder Singh on Friday said the poor donors, who were victims of the kidney trade, should not languish in jail any more. P5

Doctors must join probe today or...

TIMES NEWS NETWORK

Jalandhar: The special investigating team, probing the kidney trade racket, has decided to file an application for cancellation of bail of the three doctors and an assistant of Dr Sareen, if they do not join investigations by Saturday morning.

The three doctors who have been granted bail include Dr PK Jain (who performed the surgeries), Dr Bhupinder Sandhu and Dr Bhushan Kumar, while the assistant is Kulwinder Singh. IGP SK Sharma clarified that no media person was involved in the scam.

Speaking at a press conference following a seminar on policing here, Sharma said teams had been sent out to various states, which were mentioned in the documents of the donors and the recipients.

"So far 18 persons had been arrested and more arrests are likely in the coming days," the IGP said. "Since 1994, Dr Praveen Sareen has done 2,084 kidney transplants involving non-related donors. We are investigating 437 cases which were done after registration of the case in September 2002," said Sharma.

He added that due to number of fake addresses, the team was going to focus on establishing a nexus between donors, doctors, authorisation committee and middlemen.

PUNJAB

Kidney scam: SIT to recommend action against police officials

Names of cops not disclosed; team also to probe role of politicians

HT Correspondent
Amritsar, March 7

THE SPECIAL Investigation Team (SIT) probing the infamous multi-crore kidney scam, while reviewing its progress today, has decided to recommended action of "service misconduct" against some police officials, including two IPS officers, for their indirect involvement in the case.

Addressing mediapersons, ADGP-cum-OSD (Law and Order) A.A. Siddiqui, under whom the SIT was constituted, said no direct involvement of any police officer could be established.

He, however, admitted that certain police officers played a suspicious role in the scam and the SIT would recommend action against them.

Fielding a volley of questions, Siddiqui, however, declined to disclose the name of the police officers against whom action was being recommended. "Yes, there is involvement of three or four police officials, including one or two IPS officers. You all know their names very well," he said, adding that the role of politicians into the scam was also being looked into and those involved would not be spared.

Meanwhile, the SIT gave a clean chit to Amritsar SSP Narinderpal Singh, as Siddiqui said his name did not figure in the investigations carried out so far.

SIT incharge S.K. Sharma and member Kunwar Vijay Partap Singh were also present during the press conference.

Siddiqui said investigations into the case were almost complete, adding that they would produce the challan shortly.

Giving details of the investigations, Sharma said as many as three doctors – kidney transplant surgeon P.K. Sareen, Authorisation Committee chairman O.P. Mahajan and head of Forensic Science Department of the local medical college Jagdish Gargi – had been arrested so far.

He said some doctors, including P.K. Jain, Bhupinder Singh, Bhushan Aggarwal and Hardyal Mehta, are yet to be arrested.

He disclosed that 13 kidney donors, nine middlemen and some advocates had also been arrested, while two middlemen – Raju and Chandan – had been declared proclaimed offenders.

To a query why the recipients were not involved in the investigations, Sharma said, "Our main focus was to expose the nexus among doctors, middlemen and donors and we did not want to unnecessarily harass the recipients, who, at the time of the crisis, were being exploited by kidney transplant surgeons."

Siddiqui said the Special Investigation Team had taken up only those cases that took place after January 1, 2001, and he has directed the DIGs concerned to hold inquiries at their respective levels to probe past cases.

What about Executive Magistrates?

DIVERGENT VIEWS emerged during the press conference over the involvement of the Executive Magistrates who attested the joint affidavits of donors and recipients. IG S.K. Sharma gave a clean chit to the Executive Magistrates, pleading that they had attested the joint affidavits of donors and recipients on the condition that the same had already been verified by advocates.

However, ADGP A.A. Siddiqui said the role of the Executive Magistrates was very much under the scanner, but the problem was that they could not initiate action against civil bureaucrats. He added that only their high-ups could take action against them.

Kidney scam: addresses of 400 donors found 'fake'

Book Rajan Gupta also, demands Dang

Varinder Walia
Tribune News Service

Amritsar, January 22

All the 12 Special Investigation Teams (SIT), sent to other states to serve notices on 400 kidney donors returned 'empty handed' as their addresses were found to be 'fake'. These teams were sent from Amritsar, Hoshiarpur and Jalandhar districts to serve notices on the recipients and donors in Punjab and other states.

Talking to The Tribune, Mr S.K. Sharma, IG (Jalandhar) who heads the SIT revealed that the kidney recipients had tried to hoodwink the enforcement agencies in connivance with all concerned.

Mr Sharma, however, said that he had directed SP (City) and SIT member Kunwar Vijay Partap Singh to arrest persons concerned including recipients, middlemen and musclemen' who had allegedly kidnapped Bagicha Singh (17) from the Golden Temple and had his kidney removed at gun-point in a Jalandhar hospital. The kidney was transplanted on a police inspector of Chandigarh, after getting hair of Bagicha Singh cut. He was given the name of 'Raju', and shown as a migrant in the record and then his case was cleared by the Authorisation Committee before removing his kidney, he was kept in illegal confinement in Chandigarh and threatened if he went to the police. The victim Bagicha Singh, a resident of Muradpura (Ludhiana) met Baljit Singh of Fatehgarh Shudarchakk in the temple in February last. Baljit Singh on the pretext of making him learn driving took him to the residence of Suresh Kumar Sharma, a relative of the accused, reportedly a police inspector in Chandigarh. The victim was, however, denied the promised Rs 40,000.

Meanwhile, Mr Satya Pal Dang, senior CPI leader, sought registration of criminal case against Mr Rajan Gupta, IG for his alleged involvement in the kidney scam. In a communication to Capt Amarinder Singh, Chief Minister, Mr Dang said, "It is obvious that without some police officials helping and protecting Dr Sareen and his associates this organised crime could not have thrived, a prima facie case stands already made out against IG Rajan Gupta.

Mr Dang also sought probe into the functioning of magistrates, oath-commissioners and public notaries who had attested blatantly and clearly false affidavits. He said it must be examined to find out as to why they did that and whether it was for a consideration. If so who greased their palms — relatives of recipients of kidneys or doctor Parveen Sareen's men etc. He said law must take its own course against them too. He urged the Chief Minister to send a detailed report to the Chief Justice of Punjab and Haryana High Court on the role played by them.

HOSHIARPUR: Mr Gurmit Singh, SP (Headquarters) and member of the Special Investigation Team (SIT) formed to probe kidney scam, by Mr A.A. Saddiqui, Additional Director-General (Law and Order) and OSD to the Chief Minister under the supervision of Mr S.K. Sharma, Inspector-General Zonal Jalandhar has recorded the statements of 25 to 30 patients including two/three kidney donors so far. During investigation it was revealed that only Rs 10,000 to 40,000 had been given to each kidney donor whereas the major share of amount taken from the patients had been shared between the middlemen, and doctors. As many as 143 files of kidney patients have been given to Mr Gurmit Singh for investigation out of which 84 are from UP, Bihar, Rajasthan, Himachal Pradesh, Delhi, Mumbai and Jammu and Kashmir.

Mr Gurmit Singh said here today that letters had been issued to 84 patients, who had got transplanted kidney, for their personal appearance before him for recording of their statements. 35 letters had been received back undelivered due to fake addresses and 49 had not replied or responded so far. Besides, 87 letters had been issued to the kidney donors out of which 56 had come back due to fake addresses whereas 31 had not replied so far.

He said, during investigation donors and patients had come out against the doctors and middlemen. Further investigation was in progress, he added.

Deponent

Verification

That the contents of the above said affidavit are true and correct and no false statement is given. Attested at Amritsar.

Place: Amritsar.

LTI/-

Dated: 06.06.2000

Deponent

9/13

True Translated Copy

Advocate

10/14

no FIR registered on this affidavit

Original Affidavit of the first complaint (names hidden for security reasons)

Annexure P-25/B/T

DPH 363 **Form No. 4** 186/ 14.07.2001

Serial No. ......

Registration Unit/ Village/ Town/ Municipal Council/ Cantt/ Block/ Tehsil

Police Station .... Distt. Amritsar

1. Date of Death: 19.07.2001
2. Name of deceased:
3. Father's Name:
4. Place of Death:
5. Age: 30 years
6. Sex: Male
7. Marital Status: Bachelor/ Married/ Divorcee/ Separate/ Widow: Bachelor
8. Occupation: Labour
9. Religion: Hindu
10. Nationality: ......
11. Permanent Address
12. Cause of Death : Ailing
13. Is doctor verified? : Yes
14. If the medical help has been given, then what type of help given: Basic help.
15. Informant:
    (i) Name: V
    (ii) Address:

X X X X

Dated: 20.07.01

Seal and Sd/-

President/ Secretary, Signature / Thumb Mark of Informant/

The Marwari Shivpuri Samiti.

X X X X

True Translated Copy

Advocate

Details of one of the many illegal cremations of kidney donors who died of negligence